MARIAN BABSON

A FOOL FOR MURDER

A MYSTERY

WARNER BOOKS

A Time Warner Company

WARNER BOOKS EDITION

Cover illustration by Phillip Singer
Cover design by Jackie Merri Meyer

This Warner Books Edition is published by arrangement with
Walker and Company.

Warner Books, Inc.
666 Fifth Avenue
New York, N.Y. 10103

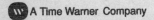 A Time Warner Company

Printed in the United States of America

First Warner Books Printing: May, 1991

10 9 8 7 6 5 4 3 2 1

CHAPTER 1

WHO'D BE A HOSTESS?

Tamar was having hysterics upstairs in her room.

Jennifer had locked herself in the library where she could be heard laughing senselessly.

Godfrey had whistled to his dog and departed for the village pub, which meant we wouldn't see him again for hours.

And it was only Friday afternoon and half the guests hadn't arrived yet.

I stood in the doorway watching Godfrey stamping down the driveway, his progress impeded by the dogs frolicking around his feet. He had whistled for his own Airedale, but the whistle had also brought Jennifer's liver-and-white King Charles spaniel and Tamar's apricot miniature French poodle rushing to him, carrying their leads in their mouths and staring up at him with hopeful, trusting eyes. Muttering under his breath, he had surrendered to the inevitable and harnessed up the lot of them. It was the easiest way of getting out of the house without being subjected to canine hysterics as well as the human variety.

Aunt Maddy had retreated to the kitchen wing, the green baize door uncompromisingly shut against all comers. It probably didn't apply to me, but I didn't feel like chancing my luck just yet. The same went for taking a stroll around the grounds—I might encounter the strange young man who was the cause of the present tension.

The problem was that Tamar was between marriages, but not between men. She had arrived with her current boy-friend and taken great exception to the fact that Aunt Maddy flatly refused to put them in the same room. She had allotted the blue guest room to Tamar and grudgingly told the boy-friend that he could sleep in the room over the garage. At that point, the balloon went up.

However, Aunt Maddy was the nominal hostess and had might, if not right, on her side. Jennifer had a warped sense of humor. Godfrey had the usual male craving for quiet and peace at any price. His sisters had always been too much for him.

Everything was too much for Cromwell. He had disappeared up the tree at the far end of the kitchen garden and could be heard howling imprecations at anyone who stepped out of the back door.

Mentally damning Jennifer for usurping the library, I went reluctantly into the drawing-room. The atmosphere still seemed to be jangling with the emotions so recently unleashed in there.

"I hate you!" Tamar had screamed at Aunt Maddy, abruptly reverting to childhood when she realized she wasn't going to get her own way. "I'll hate you for ever!'' She turned and ran from the room; we could hear her stumbling up the stairs, sobbing noisily.

"Ridiculous!" Aunt Maddy had snorted. "A grown woman of thirty-five! And that 'boy-friend'—boy, indeed! He must be fifteen years younger, at least."

"It's all the rage these days," I tried to enlighten Aunt Maddy gently. "Older women with younger men. They call them Toy Boys."

Aunt Maddy snorted again and called them something else entirely. It simply demonstrated the erosion of standards these days. Once, a woman of her generation wouldn't have admitted to knowing an expression like that, far less allow it to sully her lips.

That was when Jennifer had begun to laugh. Unable to stop she had gestured, apologetically and darted into the library.

Aunt Maddy had shaken her head and moved off towards the kitchen with a dignity that did not quite hide her anger and dismay. I knew she was convinced that she had done the right thing and she probably had. After all, it was she who would have to answer to Uncle Wilmer tomorrow. She was her brother's housekeeper and custodian of the house in his absence. He demanded perfection— and he usually got it. If he didn't, his tantrums could be far more awe-inspiring than Tamar's.

I sank into a chair and picked up one of the glossy magazines Tamar considered a necessary adjunct of rail travel, almost as indispensable as a ticket, despite any companions she might have along with her to amuse her. I had hardly opened it when the front doorbell rang insistently.

I opened the door to a pair of village urchins. They

looked up at me hopefully. "Missis," one of them said. "Missis, your cat is up a tree."

"Yes," I said. "I know."

"Well—" My calm appeared to disappoint him. "Aren't you going to do something about it? Aren't you going to call the Fire Brigade?"

"No," I said. "He's all right. He'll come down when he's ready."

"When will that be?" They were aggrieved at missing what they had thought was going to be a bit of excitement.

"About Wednesday," I said and closed the door on them firmly. It was bending the truth a bit, but it had given them the nice dramatic touch they had been anticipating. Actually, Cromwell would come down whenever he was hungry, eat his fill, and retreat up the tree again. He probably would not come down permanently and rejoin the family until Wednesday—or possibly Thursday.

Meanwhile, Uncle Wilmer would make his triumphant return home from his American lecture tour tomorrow— to the surprise party waiting to celebrate his seventieth birthday and his latest, greatest triumph.

He had departed on the tour as "Wilful Wilmer" Creighleigh, economist, ex-university don, Government adviser and, latterly, author of *A Fool and His Money*, an unexpected best-seller which had been intended as a textbook but which had taken the American market by storm—hence the hastily arranged lecture tour.

He was returning home as *Sir* Wilmer Creighleigh, having been named in the Birthday Honors List during his absence, doubtless to his intense gratification and the jubilation of his American hosts.

We were quite delighted about it ourselves, although

Who will be the victim?
Who will be the killer?

TAMAR CREIGHLEIGH: Between marriages and other entanglements, she has already done her best to turn the household upside down. Who knows how far her anger can go?

TOY BOY: He is Tamar's latest plaything, and he has already lost his Pentax camera to an irate Sir Wilmer. But the more things unravel in the house in Little Puddleton, the more Toy Boy has to gain.

GODFREY CREIGHLEIGH: He has it all figured out. His father will transfer his wealth now and avoid taxes later. The only thing Godfrey hasn't counted on is a new stepmother.

DAVINA HARDY: The neighbor and her daughter occupy a special place in the Creighleigh household. Then Davina's plans to become Lady Creighleigh are cruelly and prematurely killed.

WANDA-LU: Who would have thought it possible? The Southern belle is young enough to be Sir Wilmer's granddaughter. Now she stands to inherit a fortune—if someone doesn't get to her first.

➤   ➤

*Published by
WARNER BOOKS

Aunt Maddy had been slightly annoyed about the secrecy. "He might have warned us," she had said, after answering the telephone for the umpteenth time and informing the party at the other end that, yes, it was thrilling; yes, we were very pleased; and, no, Sir Wilmer couldn't come to the phone as he was on a lecture tour of America. "He must have known about it. They don't just bestow this sort of thing on people without any advance communication. He might have let us know. We shouldn't have had to learn about it from the newspapers."

"He probably wanted to surprise us." I had tried to soothe her ruffled feathers. "You know how he likes to spring his little surprises. And also," I had added, as she appeared singularly unsoothed, "it might have slipped his mind in the excitement of packing and writing his speeches for the lecture tour. It was all arranged so suddenly. He probably intended to tell us just before he left—and then there was that extra excitement at the airport and he was on the plane before he realized he hadn't."

"Well . . ." Against her better judgment, she had allowed herself to be convinced. There *had* been all that excitement just before he left. The book had unexpectedly soared to the top of the best-seller list in this country as well, and suddenly there were constant telephone calls and conferences and rumors of a television program of his own in the autumn. Magazines were besieging him for articles, a Sunday heavy was suggesting a weekly column, there were plans bruited of a lecture tour in this country, a paperback, bookshop appearances. Suddenly, it seemed, Uncle Wilmer was a hot property. Very hot.

Like the rest of the family, I was very pleased. Unlike

them, I was not surprised. I had typed the manuscript. Something had told me at the time that it was going to be the sort of book that either fell with a dull thud or soared to amazing success. And nothing Uncle Wilmer had tossed into the air had yet fallen with a dull thud.

It had started out to be a treatise on economics; the sort of tome that, with a bit of luck and a few friends in the right places, might be chosen as a textbook in a few universities, thus providing a steady comfortable income over the years. There would, of course, be judicious revisions every few years to keep it up to date and, incidentally, make sure students couldn't resell their books to the incoming class.

But, somewhere along the way, Uncle Wilmer's impatience and natural irascibility had taken over. The personality that had kept generations of students poised uneasily between terror and hero-worship began to come through strongly.

At first, it was just an occasional side to the sober text; then a footnote or two; until, finally, his constant irritation with the obtuseness of society in general and students in particular broke out and swamped the neatly sculptured outline he had intended to follow. He let fly: sideswiping those colleagues who were safely dead; damning with faint praise the living; divulging the secrets of commercial firms; explaining the fine line between fraud and legal business practice; even listing the ten most lucrative confidence games in order of the number of suckers falling for them. Having thus got into his stride, he pointed out the most common errors in deciphering the fine print of contracts and mortgages; why your shopping/restaurant bills were inevitably higher than you expected them to be and what you could do about it. He went on to lambast his readers for the amounts of electricity/gas/oil/fuel/energy they wasted every day and told them how to cut down on the waste.

In fact, he snarled about—if not covered completely— every possible aspect of finances today.

It might not have been economics as it was commonly thought of, but it certainly made spicy reading. When, in a final burst of spleen, he changed the title from *Modern Economics, 1925–1985 to A Fool and His Money*, it added the crowning touch.

The book had added greatly to Uncle—*Sir*—Wilmer's fortune, which had been growing apace anyway. He had gone into the Stock Market after taking early retirement from his university and proceeded to prove that he had always known what he was talking about by making several killings. Whatever else Uncle Wilmer was, *he* wasn't a fool.

The door opened cautiously and Aunt Maddy poked her head around, surveying the room before she moved into it. She crossed to the sofa, sat down and swung her feet up with a deep sigh. "I don't know," she said. "I just don't know."

"Well, *I* know someone who's going to get a copy of Debrett's *Guide to the New Etiquette* for Christmas," I said mischievously. "If Tamar is speaking to you again by then."

"Debrett's isn't what it used to be," Aunt Maddy mourned.

"Nothing is."

"Unfortunately," she corrected me, "Tamar is. That girl—woman—hasn't changed at all. I thought she'd grow wiser as she grew older—but she hasn't. She's just as headstrong, and silly with it, at thirty-five as she was at fifteen. But it's far less becoming at her present age." She sighed again. "I just don't know what to do about her."

"She's of age," I said. "There isn't anything you *can* do."

"I suppose not." Aunt Maddy hated to admit it. "But I can't help feeling that there's something I *should* do."

"I should leave it to Uncle Wilmer," I said firmly. "He's the one to do anything—if there's anything to be done."

"It's all right for you, Pippa," she complained. "You're not directly involved. There are a lot of things Will ought to do—if he ever gets around to them. He ought to face facts, for one thing. It was all very well in the old days, but there's a lot of money involved now. Tomorrow is his seventieth birthday. It's high time he took a few steps to see to a suitable provision for his children, so that they don't lose everything in Capital Transfer Tax when he goes." There was grim relish in her voice. "Like it or not, he has to face the fact that he isn't getting any younger."

"Seventy isn't so terribly old these days," I said. "Especially not for someone who's always taken care of himself the way Uncle Wilmer has."

"It's not so young, either, and it's time your Uncle Wilmer realized that."

"I'm sure he does." There were times when I could almost feel sorry for Uncle Wilmer, dominated as he was, by so many women—including, I suppose, me. When you consider everything, he put up with it very well. Not that anyone could, by any stretch of the imagination, think of him as henpecked. Nor his family as browbeaten. A draw, was more like it.

"I had a word with him before he went off to the States," Aunt Maddy said, with the air of one recalling an unpleasant duty accomplished. "Really, he should have seen to it before he left. I know that air travel is supposed to be safer than crossing the street these days, but one never can tell."

"Uncle Wilmer is a fatalist. He believes that when your number's up, it's up. Nothing you can do can make any difference."

"It can make a considerable difference to your family." I was corrected once again. "*If* you have behaved responsibly and made proper provision for them."

I began to see why Uncle Wilmer hadn't been in any too good a mood when he flew off—and why there had been that nasty scene with the Press at Heathrow. There was no use mentioning it to Aunt Maddy, however. She would never accept any of the responsibility for it.

"When are the others arriving?" It was time for a change of subject. I was not my uncle's keeper, only his secretary, and my expectations were minimal. I was not prepared to get into a discussion about what might or might not be due to my cousins.

"Jarvis is coming down from London after the bank closes this afternoon. Reggie and Flora are driving down tomorrow. And I'm not sure when Ian Trifflin will arrive—" Aunt Maddy paused significantly. "But your uncle especially asked that he be here."

"The Triffid?" In my astonishment, I reverted to the childhood nickname.

"Wilmer was most insistent that his solicitor should be present this weekend, so I invited Mr. Trifflin to the birthday celebration," Aunt Maddy said complacently. "That's why I'm sure Wilmer has thought over my advice and is taking it."

It was possible, I supposed, but rather unlikely that Uncle Wilmer would be so quick off the mark immediately upon his return home. It would take at least the weekend for his jet-lag to wear off; it was most unlike him to want to get down to business matters so quickly.

Unless something had happened to him in the States to jolt him into a greater awareness of his mortality than Aunt Maddy's little lecture might have done. Uneasily, I wondered if he had had a heart attack—or "a coronary incident," as his hosts would have termed it. He *had* been driving himself quite hard in the weeks prior to his departure.

Aunt Maddy was untroubled by any such fears, however, and it would be unkind to put them into her mind. We would know the worst soon enough and she had enough problems at the moment with her houseful of family and guests.

"I suppose he'll have to join us for meals," she sighed.

For a moment, I was lost, then my mind managed to make the quantum leap necessary to catch up with her. She was not begrudging food to Uncle Wilmer, nor even to Ian Trifflin. It was Tamar's Toy Boy she had gone back to fretting about.

"We can't very well leave his dinner out on the backstep beside Cromwell's," I pointed out.

"No." Her sigh was regretful. Plainly, this was just

the sort of treatment she considered suitable, but she didn't quite dare. "I refuse to sit them beside each other," she warned. "Goodness knows what they'd get up to. He can sit at the far end of the table."

Below the salt. It was in the best tradition. I began to feel almost sorry for whatever his name was—I hadn't quite caught it. I wondered if he'd had any idea what he was letting himself in for when he accepted Tamar's invitation for a quiet weekend with the family.

"Wilmer *will* be upset. I don't know how I'm going to tell him. At his age, and after such a long, tiring trip, he shouldn't have to come back to family problems."

"Let Tamar tell him," I advised. It's *her* friend. Anyway, Uncle Wilmer ought to be so chuffed about his knighthood that nothing could bother him."

"But if the Press got hold of it, they'd use it to make him look a fool. You *know* they'll be gunning for him more than ever now."

"It's his own fault," I said heartlessly. "Sometimes he seems to go out of his way to antagonize them. Anyway, he can't be held responsible for what his family does. Tamar's of age—and then some."

"But is that boy?" Aunt Maddy would not be comforted. "He looks awfully young to me. He may be even younger than we think he is. I suppose we couldn't ask—?"

"No, we couldn't. Remember, eighteen is the coming-of-age point these days—" Not in this house, though. Uncle Wilmer had resolutely ignored the nuances of my eighteenth birthday two years ago and given me a new coat and a book token. And I wouldn't come into my full inheritance from my father's estate until I was twenty-five.

"Anyway," I said, "it's only for the weekend. After that, they'll be back in London where no one will raise an eyebrow."

"I wouldn't be too sure of that," Aunt Maddy said. "There are still plenty of respectable people left in this world—even in London."

Just as I felt that this conversation was getting out of hand, the doorbell rang. We both leaped to answer it, grateful for the diversion. My relief was short-lived.

Toy Boy stood on the doorstep.

CHAPTER 2

"SPEAK OF THE DEVIL!" AUNT MADDY SAID UNDER her breath. I hoped he hadn't heard her.

"Sorry to disturb you." Toy Boy tried an ingratiating smile which faltered and faded as he met Aunt Maddy's eyes. "I thought I'd collect Tamar and we might go somewhere for a drink. If it's all right with you, that is."

"Tamar is in her room," Aunt Maddy said with such finality that it sounded as though Tamar might never emerge again.

"You haven't locked her in?" He looked as though he'd believe anything of us.

"Certainly not," Aunt Maddy said. "Tamar is a grown woman."

"That was what I thought—until we got here," he muttered.

"*What*?" Aunt Maddy snapped.

"That was what I thought—" he began to repeat, but Aunt Maddy stopped him. That wasn't what she had meant.

"*What*," she demanded, "is that—that *thing* around your neck?"

"It's a camera," he said, then seemed to feel that the answer was so obvious it might not be what she was driving at. "A Hassenblad—the best there is," he explained.

"Oh, nooo!" Aunt Maddy wailed. "No!"

"No?" He stepped back nervously, one hand went up to hover protectively in front of his camera.

"No," Aunt Maddy said firmly. "You can't use that here. I'd suggest you put it away for the weekend. Sir Wilmer would be most upset if he saw it. He hates cameras. He even smashed a few at the airport when he was flying to the States."

"I know," the boy said. "One of them was my Pentax. That was how I met Tamar. She was the only one seeing him off who had the decency to come over and apologize to us for his behavior."

"Well, you're likely to get that one smashed, too, if Sir Wilmer sees it here," Aunt Maddy said, "with more truth than tact.

"That wouldn't surprise me," he said. "If you ask me, the old boy's barking mad."

"As it happens," Aunt Maddy said icily, "I did *not* ask you."

"You'd better call Tamar, hadn't you?" I nudged Aunt Maddy, edging her back from the door. She was in a mood to slam it in Toy Boy's face, but she could not be allowed to. She had already been rude enough. After all, the boy *was* Tamar's guest.

"I'll call her." Aunt Maddy moved away reluctantly, obviously suspecting—rightly—that I was going to invite him inside the house as soon as her back was turned. Well, we couldn't leave him standing on the doorstep, could we? Aunt Maddy could. I couldn't.

"Come in," I said traitorously, as soon as I heard her footsteps fading. "You can wait for Tamar in the drawing-room."

"You're sure I won't contaminate the place?" But he stepped inside anyway. "You don't want me to take my shoes off first, or something?"

"No," I said, "but you *had* better hide that camera before Sir Wilmer gets back."

"So everybody keeps telling me." He looked around the room and then perched on the edge of a chair, as though ready for instant flight. "I just want to take some background photos today. Don't worry, I'll be careful when the old boy is around. I'm not letting him ruin another camera on me. Cost a fortune, they do."

"If he does," I warned, "we won't be responsible."

"No—" He gave me a lazy, half-contemptuous smile. "None of you are ever responsible, are you? It must be a comfortable existence."

"It is." I wouldn't give him the satisfaction of rising to the bait. What stories had Tamar been telling him of her home life? Not the truth, certainly. That wouldn't be nearly dramatic enough for Tamar.

"You're the adopted one, aren't you?"

That gave me a clue. "No," I said. "Actually, I'm

not. I'm Sir Wilmer's niece, his younger sister's child, a blood relative. There was never any question of adoption—there was no need for it.''

"Don't get shirty." But a certain uneasiness showed at the back of his eyes. "I got the wrong end of the stick, that's all."

"Is it?" I doubted that. Tamar had obviously been embroidering again. I wondered how much else she had treated with similar artistic license. From the look in his eyes, so did he.

A rush of footsteps on the stairs saved us from further awkward revelations. Tamar flung herself into the room and into Toy Boy's arms. It struck me that he was a bit slow about catching her.

"Angel!" she exclaimed. "You've stormed the barricades to rescue me!"

"Yeah . . . well . . ." Aunt Maddy had entered the room behind her and Toy Boy unhanded Tamar with as much alacrity as though it had been demanded by an avenging hero. "I thought we might go down to the local and have a drink. If there is such a thing as a pub in this godforsaken hole."

"Angel, of course there is! And—" she turned ostentatiously to face me—"you can tell *her* not to worry. We'll be back in good time for dinner."

"And you can tell your Cousin Tamar—" Quick to take up the challenge, Aunt Maddy also routed her remarks through me—"I never worry that she or any of her *friends* will miss a free meal!"

I wished they wouldn't do that. But there was no point in wishing. They'd done it all their lives. Behind me, I heard the almost-silent snick of a latch turning and knew that Jennifer was listening to see if it was safe to enter the arena. No fool, she.

"Look—" Toy Boy appeared to be doing some wishing of his own. He obviously wished he was back having a quiet pint in some King's Road pub—or even having another camera demolished at Heathrow. "Look, I can afford—"

"Angel, that isn't the point!" Tamar mimed a kiss at him. "And *she* knows it! Now, let's be off." She looked around. "Where's Frou-Frou?"

"At the pub already," I said. "Godfrey took her with the other dogs when he went down."

"Oh, good!" Tamar said. Toy Boy looked as though he might like to say something else. "We'll link up with them there, then." She started for the door, then stopped and looked back at Toy Boy, still rooted to the spot. He must have led a sheltered life. It was obvious that he had never encountered anyone like Aunt Maddy before and, so far as he was concerned, she would do until the real Medusa stood up.

"*Come* along," Tamar ordered, in much the same tone she would have used to Frou-Frou. She sailed out of the room without waiting to check that she had been obeyed.

It might have given her pause to look back. For a split second, Toy Boy abruptly looked less like a toy. Briefly, something ugly flashed across his face and was gone. He looked after Tamar thoughtfully, then glanced down at the camera on his chest. It seemed to recall him to order.

"Right," he said, although Tamar had not waited for a reply. He followed her docilely from the room.

"Oh dear!" Looking after them, Aunt Maddy just

stopped short of wringing her hands. "I don't know what your Uncle Wilmer will say, I'm sure."

"Something ripe and to the point." I *was* sure. It would not be the first time Uncle Wilmer had dealt with Tamar's aberrations. At least she was not tied to this one legally—yet. "He'll probably threaten to cut her out of his will again."

"Oh, I *hope* we're not going to have more scenes!" Aunt Maddy gave up and wrung her hands in earnest. "You don't suppose he's already heard about it, do you?" She was struck by an unwelcome new thought. "He made such a point of asking me to have his solicitor here. The minute he returns, not even waiting a few days to get over his jetlag. Oh, he must be furious!"

"We don't know that he knows." It was negative comfort, but it was the best I could do. "It may be about something else entirely. He's probably collected a few new contracts in America and wants them vetted before he signs them."

It was plausible, even possible. With a great deal of money at stake, Uncle Wilmer wouldn't want to lose any time. Aunt Maddy began to cheer up.

Behind me, the library door closed almost soundlessly. Jennifer didn't believe it, either, and she wasn't going to come out and get into the middle of the situation. Trust Jennifer. If she were a cat, she'd be up in the topmost branches beside Cromwell.

"I suppose I ought to go back and see if Mrs. Keyes needs any help in the kitchen," Aunt Maddy said in a faintly despairing tone. "She hates it so when there are extras for dinner. And we're having so many extras all weekend. She'll be in a foul mood."

"If there's anything I can do—" I offered unenthusiastically. No one else would be likely to offer. If I were smart, I'd take a leaf from Jennifer's book and get out of the way. I could always claim that I had a lot of work to catch up on, but the truth was that I had everything fairly well under control. I'd answered all the correspondence I could handle by myself and the rest was in an orderly pile on Uncle Wilmer's desk, awaiting his own inimitable touch.

The doorbell cut through my words.

"Oh heavens!" Aunt Maddy looked haunted. "There can't be more of them arriving already!"

"It's probably just more of the local children." I started for the door. "Cromwell is terrorizing the village again." Cromwell always chose a tree bordering on the road and proclaimed his woes to all who would listen. He usually collected an audience of sympathetic children who were certain we had been mistreating him in some obscure way. The local adults were more cynical about his complaints and Mrs. Murphy, across the road, was downright hostile. Cromwell had earned his name when, as a kitten, he had knocked over the statues and vases comprising her outdoor shrine.

It was an act that had won Cromwell, an undying place in Uncle Wilmer's heart. "That cat raised the tone of the entire village at a stroke!" he often boasted. Actually, it had been several strokes. When she had tried to rebuild the grotto, he had knocked it down again—and again—until she had finally given up and confined her devotions to the inside of her house. Since when, Cromwell could do no wrong in Uncle Wilmer's eyes.

However, the child at the door was neither anxious nor

even aware that Cromwell was at it again. Furthermore, she was accompanied by her mother.

"Oh, Lynette, Davina . . ." I opened the door wider to our next-door neighbors. "Come in."

"We thought you might like these to welcome the homecoming hero." Davina proffered a bouquet of yellow roses. Lynette carried a sheaf of multicolored peonies. Like her mother, she held them out to me. I heard Aunt Maddy give a sniff in the background.

"How kind of you." I accepted the peonies but was rather more wary of the roses. Davina's roses always seemed to have an inordinate amount of thorns.

"I'll arrange them, if you like." I needn't have worried, Davina was in no hurry to give them up. "You must have a lot to do right now." Unerringly, she headed for the cubbyhole under the stairs where we kept vases, trugs, secateurs and other light floral gardening equipment.

Not wasting any time, is she? Aunt Maddy met my eyes eloquently across the room, but Lynette had followed me into the drawing-room, so we couldn't speak.

"Aren't these pretty, Lynette," I said. "Did you pick them yourself?"

She nodded gravely, a solemn child, not given to babbling, which was why Uncle Wilmer allowed her more or less the run of the house. Uncle Wilmer suffered children no more gladly than he suffered fools.

I, too, was fairly quiet, which was why I had always got along well with him—better than his own children, I had sometimes suspected. Perhaps that was why they had grown up the way they had: Godfrey so stodgy, Tamar so wild, each looking for approval or attention in their own way. Only Jennifer had seemed to realize early on that she was never going to please her father, so she might as well please herself and make at least one person happy. She had gone off and made a successful career as a television producer and now, of course, Uncle Wilmer considered her the only child who had not failed him.

By the time I had come along, he had got over the first fine flush of experimentation with young minds. Also, theories had changed, and he had become increasingly engrossed in the economic experiments which had made him so wealthy. Then, of course, I wasn't directly descended from him; I was only a niece instead of a daughter and his expectations were lower.

"Mummy picked the roses," Lynette said shyly, telling us a secret. "She said Uncle Will would like roses."

"I'm sure he will," I said warmly, covering Aunt Maddy's sniff. "And the peonies, too. How clever of you to think of them."

"I like them." Lynette lifted her head and smiled at the peonies. "They don't smell so pretty, but they're nice."

"Indeed, they are," I cut in quickly as Aunt Maddy seemed about to say something else. "Shall we go and find something pretty to put them in?"

Lynette nodded and we started for the door, but nearly collided with her mother, who was entering with two beautiful and eminently suitable vases.

"Over here, I think." Davina set the vases down on the coffee table in front of the fireplace and proceeded to fill them deftly, taking the peonies from me. "We'll have the peonies here and the roses in the entrance hall where they'll be the first thing Sir Wilmer sees when he comes in."

Thereby reminding him instantly of her. He had never been able to grow that particular shade of rose, although he had tried. Even using a cutting from Davina's bush had not worked. There was just that minute difference in the soil of the two gardens that made it impossible. Uncle Wilmer would know who had brought him the birthday roses.

"That's very kind of you, Davina," Aunt Maddy said drily. "I'm sure Wilmer will appreciate it."

"It's the least we can do," Davina said warmly. "Sir Wilmer has always been such a good neighbor to us." She stepped back to admire her own flower arrangement and her gaze rose to the portrait of Aunt Nora hanging over the mantel. She frowned slightly and looked away.

Aunt Maddy met my eyes. The portrait of Uncle Wilmer's late wife would be the first thing consigned to the attic if Davina ever became the new mistress of the house. We had long had our suspicions that that was the position she was angling for. Now that Uncle Wilmer had acquired a title, as well as the fortune he had already amassed, he was in double jeopardy. It was obvious that Davina was going to redouble her efforts and no holds would be barred.

My money was on Uncle Wilmer. He was a wily old fox and I had watched him elude many snares over the past ten years. It was a game he enjoyed and, as he had often pointed out, he was scrupulously fair: he never promised, or even hinted at, marriage. If ladies wished to leap to conclusions, that was their problem—as they eventually discovered.

"Uncle Wilmer's going to bring me a surprise," Lynette confided to us. She was the only female unlikely to be disappointed by Uncle Wilmer. He usually brought her back a little trinket, even from a trip to London.

"You mustn't say things like that, Lynette," her mother reproved her. "It isn't nice."

"But he *is*," Lynette insisted. "You said so."

"No, no, darling, I didn't say *that*," Davina protested, oddly flustered. "I said, wouldn't it be lovely to have him back again? And *you* have a nice surprise for *him*, haven't you?"

"Yes." Lynette nodded gravely. "I've learned a poem for him." She planted her feet firmly, raised her head and began to declaim—

"Under the wide and starry sky."

"No! No, darling—" Davina interrupted frantically. *"That's* not the one! That's the one you learned for elocution class. You want to recite the one I taught you. You remember: *I must go down to the sea again—*"

"I hope she remembers that tomorrow," Aunt Maddy said tartly. So did I.

Dig the grave and let me lie was hardly a sentiment Uncle Wilmer could be expected to appreciate at his seventieth birthday party. Not even after a long and exhausting American tour.

"Of course she will," Davina said, giving her darling daughter a grim look. "Now you must tell me if there's anything more I can do to help. Anything at all."

"Thank you, Davina," Aunt Maddy said, "but I think we have everything well in hand. I *have* run this household for the past fifteen years—" *Without your help* hung unspoken in the air.

"Oh yes, of course." Davina smiled with excessive charm, well aware that a warning shot had just been fired across her bow. "But, I meant, this is such a *special* occasion: the family-and-*intimate*-friends party tomorrow and then the big party for *everyone* on Sunday. And you have so many guests coming. If there's anything at all I can do, you mustn't hesitate to call on me."

"Thank you, Davina, that's very kind of you."

"And you, Pippa—" Davina turned to me. "I know Sir Wilmer keeps you busy. The postman told me he's been delivering tapes from the States all the time Sir Wilmer has been away. If you need any help with the typing—"

"Thank you," I said. "It's all done. I type them as they come in, you know." Did she really imagine I left everything to the last minute? "Everything is ready and waiting for him."

"Oh, that's fine," Davina said. She plucked at the peonies, rearranging them in the bowl. It was becoming obvious that she could not prolong her visit, since we were not in a gossiping mood and, as she herself had observed, we had work to do.

"If you'd really like to be of help—" I relented slightly, ignoring Aunt Maddy's sudden glare.

"Yes?" Davina looked up brightly.

"You might give a thought for Uncle Wilmer's main problem of the moment. He can't decide on the title for his new book. He's torn between *Fools' Gold* and *Fools Rush In*."

"*Fools' Gold* or *Fools Rush In*." Davina repeated the proposed titles appreciatively. "Yes, yes, I can see the problem. They're both quite good, aren't they? And they carry out the *Fools* theme he introduced in his first book . . ."

She was looking a lot happier and Aunt Maddy had relaxed. This was something Davina could do out of the house. Furthermore, it would take some of the strain off the rest of us when Uncle Wilmer wished to debate the question. Davina could quite happily spend hours arguing obscure points with Uncle Wilmer, whereas the rest of us tended to have a lower threshold of boredom. Of course, we hadn't Davina's interest in Uncle Wilmer.

"Yes, I'll have to think that over very carefully. Of course, Sir Wilmer can always use one of them for the next book, but that doesn't solve the problem of which one is most appropriate for *this* book. Perhaps I could make a list of the pros and cons . . ."

"Why don't you do that?" It was a strong hint from Aunt Maddy. "I'm sure Wilmer will appreciate it."

"Yes," Davina said, with sudden resolution. "Yes. If there's nothing I can do here to help, I'll go and get started on that. Come along, Lynette." She headed for the door.

"And you might give Lynette a bit more rehearsal . . ." Aunt Maddy unkindly called after them.

CHAPTER 3

"I HOPE WILL HAS MORE SENSE THAN TO MARRY THAT woman!" Aunt Maddy pushed the coffee table back into position, a faint pink flush of irritation coloring her porcelain complexion. Davina was always subtly nudging the furniture into what she considered better positions, which was not only tactless but downright stupid of her. It signalled all too clearly that, once installed as mistress of the house, she would institute a wholesale rearrangement, both of furniture and of lives.

Aunt Maddy would be the first to go. Davina would not want a resident housekeeper around who might challenge her authority as chatelaine. Especially not Uncle Wilmer's sister.

I would probably be allowed to stay on as secretary— but not living in the house. Davina had already suggested to me that a young girl must find it "confining" to live with elderly relatives and didn't I think I'd be happier renting a room in the village to which I could retire at the end of the day? It would, she had pointed out quite correctly, if a trifle chillingly, put an end to being "on duty" twenty-four hours a day. With such an arrangement, I could work a proper nine-to-five secretarial day, and have evenings and weekends to myself. She didn't specify what I might do with evenings and weekends alone in a place like Little Puddleton.

There might not be so much room for "the children," either. Davina might reluctantly accept that adult stepchildren were part of the price she had to pay for becoming Lady Creighleigh, but it was a fair bet that she'd do everything she could to ease them out of the picture as much as possible. She had already softly insinuated that, surely, it was excessive for each of them to have a room kept ready for them. Especially as this was a house Wilmer had bought in later years, when his fortunes were on the upswing, and had never been their childhood home. One "family" guest room ought to do for all three of them; their visits rarely coincided, except at Christmas, and the space might otherwise be used to good advantage. Say, a guest suite for housing the important people like the celebrities and foreign publishers now playing an increasing part in Wilmer's life.

"Oh, I don't think he'd *marry* her." Belatedly, I realized Aunt Maddy was waiting for some sort of answer—preferably a reassuring one. "But I suppose you can't blame her for hoping."

"Hoping?" Aunt Maddy snorted. "She's done everything but measure up for new curtains while Will's been gone. You don't imagine he might have *committed* himself before he left, do you?"

"If he had, she'd never have been able to keep it to herself all this time." That much, I was sure of. "But I know they had an evening together, just the two of them, a couple of days before he left on his tour. He might have got sentimental over the wine and said something she misinterpreted. He was in an odd mood those last few days . . ."

"Sentimental? That's one word for it!" Aunt Maddy sniffed. She had a fine range of respiratory noises and the measure of her annoyance was the frequency with which she used them. "I don't like it. He's an old man, and he wouldn't be the first to be so flattered by the attentions of a young woman that he got himself in deeper than he intended. I suppose it will be left to us to unpick the whole thing."

"Seventy isn't all that old these days," I protested. "And Davina isn't all that young. She must be close to forty."

"That's still a lot younger than he is," Aunt Maddy said uncompromisingly. "And she's not nearly intelligent enough for Will, few people are. But she's quite attractive, I'll grant you that."

"And Uncle Wilmer is very fond of little Lynette." All in all, it wouldn't be such a bad match—except for the way it would disturb the *status quo*. That factor would count with Uncle Wilmer as much as with Aunt Maddy. His circumstances were extremely comfortable and had been for quite some time. He would not want the household disrupted, especially not at a time when he was anxious to settle down after his travels and get on with his new book. That would weigh more heavily in his consideration than any amount of pressure from Davina. In fact, she would damage her own chances if she pushed him too hard.

"I wouldn't worry about it," I said. "It may never happen."

"I wouldn't, ordinarily," Aunt Maddy said. "If it weren't for the way Davina has been behaving lately. I wish she didn't live next door. There's no denying that gives her the inside track."

"Oh, come now—" Jennifer spoke from the doorway, having obviously decided things were quiet enough for her to emerge from her sanctuary. "That's putting it a bit strong. You make it sound as though desperate females were being trampled in the race to carry off Father. He's not that much of a prize, you know."

"Perhaps not, but he wouldn't appreciate you saying so." Aunt Maddy turned to face Jennifer. "It would be a good idea for you to watch your tongue this weekend, my girl."

"You mean he'll cut me out of his famous will?" Jennifer drawled. "Try frightening Tamar with that one. She's got more to lose than I have."

"Yes—" Aunt Maddy was reminded of a more pertinent problem. "And when your father sees what she's taken up with now, she probably will."

"I wouldn't worry too much about it," Jennifer said. "I don't think that's what Father has in mind."

"I wouldn't be too sure of that," I warned her. "He especially asked to have The Triffid here waiting for him tomorrow."

"*You're* all right, Pippa." Annoyingly, Jennifer dismissed my right to have any concern in the matter. "Your inheritance is assured. You'll come into the money your parents left in just another five years. You needn't worry about Father's financial arrangements."

There was left, hanging in the air, the implication that I had already done quite well out of Uncle Wilmer. He had taken me into his home after the death of my parents, fed me, clothed me and treated me as another daughter. It was not that my cousins begrudged me my place in the family. It was, perhaps, just a trace of jealousy brought on by the feeling that I had had an easier time of it than they had. There was also the normal family friction that surfaced at odd moments, especially in times of stress. And there was no doubt that this was going to be a rather stressful weekend.

"Please, Jennifer—" Aunt Maddy said uneasily. "Things are difficult enough at the moment. Don't you start, too."

What was true of me was also true of Aunt Maddy. She had been taken under Uncle Wilmer's wing—and roof—after the death of her husband fifteen years ago.

Aunt Nora had been dead a couple of years by then and Uncle Wilmer was beginning to feel the need of someone who could keep his house in order without making any emotional claims on him—he was not yet ready for that. Instead, he had turned his energies to the Stock Market and begun building the investment portfolio that was the basis of his fortune. Thus, Aunt Maddy had shared very few of his lean years and all of his affluent ones. She was the more sensitive about this since my advent had marked the dividing line between the two eras. Whereas she had tried to earn her keep by acting as housekeeper and hostess, there had been money from my parents' estate to pay my way. Any vague insinuations Jennifer made of me might also be intended for Aunt Maddy.

"I'm sorry—" Jennifer crossed over to hug Aunt Maddy reassuringly. "I'm a bit on edge, too. Everything was shaping up so well, and Tamar has to bring along her latest to *flaunt* in Father's face. It could upset everything. Just when Godfrey had got him thinking about some sensible arrangements. You know how Father is."

"What—" Aunt Maddy ignored the window dressing and went straight to the crux of the matter—"what arrangements?"

"Godfrey spoke to Father before he left on the tour. They had quite a long talk and I must say Father took it extremely well. After all, even he had to agree that seventy was some sort of a watershed. I joined them later and he spoke about it quite openly. He said he'd give the idea his deepest consideration. And—" Jennifer finished triumphantly—"since he's asked for Mr. Trifflin to be here, he obviously has!"

Aunt Maddy and I exchanged glances. Neither of us liked the sound of this.

"What idea?" I asked, one jump ahead of Aunt Maddy.

"Well, Father *is* seventy tomorrow. Heaven knows, he may live for another twenty years—and we hope he does. We made that quite clear. On the other hand, anything might happen, especially as he's travelling so much these days—and you *know* how he hates the thought of the Government stepping in and scooping up so much money before the heirs get any—"

"Will has always hated Death Duties," Aunt Maddy agreed.

"They call it Capital Transfer Tax now," Jennifer said. "But it amounts to the same thing. The only way to avoid it or minimize it, is to begin sharing out the money to the limit allowed without being liable for Transfer Tax. If Father begins now, he has every chance of being able to pass over a great deal of the money to us before . . . anything happens."

"It used to be so much simpler," Aunt Maddy said wistfully. "Once, he could have just made over everything and then lived the seven years beyond that date so that the money wasn't taxable."

"It's still rather that way," Jennifer said. "The difference now is that he can't hand over the whole lot at once—but he can make yearly payments. Then everything we received ten years before his death is nontaxable." She frowned. "Really, we should have started this five or ten years ago."

"There wasn't so much money to worry about then," I reminded her. "Otherwise, you do seem to have done all your homework on this." I now understood why Uncle Wilmer had been in such a thoroughly foul mood at the airport.

"Godfrey did most of it," Jennifer admitted. "Then he talked it over with Tamar and me. Godfrey's been worrying about it for quite some time."

That would have gone down well with Uncle Wilmer, too. The wonder was that it was only a few cameras he smashed.

Still, he must have cooled down by now since he had specifically requested the Triffid's presence. Undoubtedly, six weeks of being lionized in the States would have soothed him and cheered him and put him in a more optimistic frame of mind. He was quite probably planning his reply to the Queen's Message for his hundredth birthday celebrations.

"Well," Aunt Maddy said grudgingly, "I suppose it *is* the sensible thing to do. Although—" her eyes gleamed briefly—"I can tell you it won't be a popular move in *some* quarters."

"Precisely." Jennifer grinned impishly. "I wouldn't be surprised if our own dear Davina's ardor cooled considerably when she discovers Father is signing over large annual amounts to his children. It could solve two problems at once."

We burst into spontaneous laughter, perhaps tinged with hysteria. Seventy *was* a watershed, the old Biblical three-score-and-ten boundary of mortality. Uncle Wilmer had reached it—would reach it tomorrow—and he was not the only one who had to face the fact that we could not rely upon having him with us indefinitely.

The front door slammed and Aunt Maddy stopped laughing.

"Oh dear," she said, instantly identifying it as a bad-tempered slam. "*Now* what?"

There was a jingling in the front hall, as of excited dogs being released from leashes, and Nell Gwynn bounded into the room to frisk around Jennifer's ankles.

Godfrey followed, obviously fuming, with Rex at his heels. Rex was the only one behaving with any dignity. He walked over to the fireplace and sat down beside it, dissociating himself from everything and everyone. He had a lot in common with Cromwell.

"Oh dear," Aunt Maddy sighed again, as Godfrey stormed over to the drinks trolley and poured himself a hefty Scotch. "Is something wrong, Godfrey?"

He gulped at his drink, not answering her.

"Godfrey, dear—" Aunt Maddy looked around uneasily. "Where's Frou-Frou?"

"Frou-Frou!" Godfrey choked on his drink. "Stupid name for a dog—even that dog! How do you think I feel, walking that? Calling it? Here, Frou-Frou! Heel, Frou-Frou! Makes me feel like a ponce!"

"Yes, Godfrey. But—" Aunt Maddy refused to be diverted—"where *is* Frou-Frou?"

"With Tamar, of course!" Godfrey snapped. "She came down to the pub. Walked right in with that—that *plaything* of hers!"

"Toy Boy," I said automatically.

"That's what I said!" he snarled. "She walked right into the pub with him, brazen as brass. Now the whole village knows. Naturally, I had to leave."

"They'd know soon enough, anyway," I said. It wouldn't come as any great surprise to them. They were accustomed to Tamar by now. They viewed her with more equanimity than the family did. But then, they didn't have to deal with the repercussions. They were probably already happily making book on what those repercussions would be when Uncle Wilmer discovered the situation. Rather, they'd start making book as soon as Tamar left the pub.

"This settles it—" Godfrey spoke over our heads to Jennifer, obviously continuing a conversation they had had before. "Tamar's money will have to go into some sort of trust fund, where those—those—*creatures* of hers will never be able to get their hands on any of it."

"You may be right—" Jennifer bent over to stroke Nell Gwynn. "Tamar won't like it, though."

"Tamar will have to lump it, then." Godfrey glared at her. "She's obviously going to have to be protected for her own good. If she's like this now, what's she going to be like in another twenty or thirty years? She isn't likely to improve with age, you know. That sort doesn't."

"Nevertheless—" Jennifer murmured.

I knew what she meant. Tamar, so far, had never allowed her emotions and her finances to become entangled. None of my cousins had. There was too much of Uncle Wilmer in them for that.

"You might wait until you get it before you begin disposing of your father's money," Aunt Maddy said. She added wickedly, "There's such a thing as counting chickens before they're hatched. He won't be here until tomorrow—and he's flying. After all, planes *do* crash."

"Don't say things like that!" Godfrey splashed more Scotch into his glass. Jennifer shuddered and moved over to join him. The Scotch she poured was as large as his.

"It's something to bear in mind, just the same." Aunt

Maddy watched them disapprovingly. "What would happen to all your great plans if he never got here?"

"Don't even think about it!" Jennifer said. Involuntarily, both she and Godfrey glanced upwards, as though some malevolent fate might be hovering above waiting to swoop on and carry out ideas flung carelessly into the air.

"All right." Aunt Maddy was trying not to let her amusement show. "But you'd both better watch your step—" She could not resist twisting the knife. "Wilmer will be exhausted and jet-lagged when he gets home tomorrow. Ian Trifflin or not, it wouldn't be wise of you to let him know how much you're taking for granted. And I wouldn't advise trying to crowd him, either. You know perfectly well that, if you annoy him enough, he's quite capable of leaving everything he has to Cromwell."

"He wouldn't do that!" But Godfrey had gone pale.

"Don't be silly," Jennifer said. "Of course, he wouldn't. Father has too much respect for money to play with it like that."

"You may be right," Aunt Maddy conceded. "Cromwell *was* a bit far-fetched. On the other hand, there's always Davina . . ."

CHAPTER 4

DINNER THAT EVENING WAS NOT A SUCCESS. THE ATMO-
sphere was strained, the soup wasn't. I averted my eyes
from the sight of a long thread of celery streaming from
the corner of Toy Boy's mouth and pretended great
interest in the conversation on the other side of me while
Toy Boy raised his napkin for the fourth time in as many
mouthfuls and tried to cope.

"Yes, Pippa!" Jarvis Fortescue courteously inclined
his head towards me, obviously under the mistaken
impression that I had something to contribute to the
conversation. He had earlier lifted one spoonful of the
soup, with a pained expression regarded the threads
dangling from it like a Portuguese Man-o'-War, and
lowered it into his bowl again, declining the battle.

"Did you have a pleasant journey down?" Too late, I
realized that I had turned to him just as silence had
fallen. I threw out the conversational hook inanely. We
had already discussed his uneventful journey.

"Very pleasant, thank you." Nevertheless, he seemed
grateful for the query, or perhaps for the chance to turn
away from Tamar, who had resumed sulking. She had not
had much to say, in any case, but had confined her few

remarks to Jarvis in order to avoid speaking to Aunt Maddy, who was on her other side.

"It might have been awkward—" Carefully, he refrained from giving any indication that he considered his present situation awkward, although he could not have been unaware of undercurrents in the atmosphere. "However, I keep my car radio tuned to a commercial station and was forewarned in good time that a lorry had shed its load—strawberries, I believe—and created a traffic jam . . . sorry, no pun intended . . . along the route I had planned to take. Therefore, I took an alternate route and arrived without experiencing any inconvenience. Most useful, these commercial stations."

"Aren't they?" Aunt Maddy leaned forward, ignoring Tamar, to join in the conversation. "I wasn't sure I approved when they first started, but they *do* have some excellent programs. And most of the commercials aren't obtrusive. In any case, they're very short and, if there's one I dislike, I can always switch off."

"That's right," Godfrey agreed. "They've come a long way since Radio Caroline."

"Radio Noah's Ark, more like!" Toy Boy said. "The new pirate stations are where it's at, these days. A couple of my mates run one. They reckon to lose a transmitter every two or three weeks. Depends on how long it takes the Detector Van to catch up with—"

He stopped abruptly, having incautiously looked around and encountered Aunt Maddy's steely gaze. He, too, was broadcasting without a license.

There was another silence, during which Mrs. Keyes came in to clear away the soup plates and serve the main course. The sight of Jarvis Fortescue's untouched soup did nothing to improve her temper. She loaded her tray and bore it back to the kitchen with much unnecessary rattling of crockery. We would be lucky to get through the evening without any broken dishes.

When she returned and set the bubbling casserole before Aunt Maddy, it was with an air of defiance. We were going to have a crown roast of lamb for the family birthday celebrations tomorrow—just let anyone *dare* to complain about what she had chosen to cook for us tonight!

Not even Aunt Maddy dared. It was not what she had ordered, but she knew better than to complain right now. She sniffed audibly, but didn't actually say anything. Not even while Mrs. Keyes slammed the stack of plates down beside the casserole. She winced again, but that wasn't actually saying anything. Mrs. Keyes had her own code and did not react to unspoken criticism; anything less than the spoken word could be ignored. It took actual speech to goad her into an explosion. She had not had a good fight since Uncle Wilmer had left and was obviously boiling up for a major scene as soon as he gave her the slightest provocation.

Uncle Wilmer, tired, jet-lagged and suffering withdrawal symptoms from the abrupt loss of the extravagant adulation he would have enjoyed on his tour, would not be long in obliging her. It was not going to be a peaceful weekend.

Tight-lipped, Aunt Maddy began dishing up. The silence continued. I risked another glance at Tamar and found her glaring at me, which was most unfair. It wasn't my fault that I was sitting beside Toy Boy. Aunt Maddy had done the seating. We all knew that the placement was designed to underline the fact that I was closer to his age than Tamar was. Neither of us could help that.

"I do so hope the weather holds fine for the weekend." Jennifer beamed her most fetching smile across the table. Jarvis Fortescue was her father's bank manager. "It makes all the difference."

"Indeed, it does," he responded smoothly, as willing to spend the next twenty minutes discussing the weather as detailing his journey down from London. "Although I must say Little Puddleton has certain attractions, even in the rain."

"I always think—" Aunt Maddy passed a dish along the table, only the slightest tremor of her hand betraying her fury at having to do so, this had not been intended as a meal *en famille*; Mrs. Keyes should have served up in the kitchen—"I always think that, on a rainy day, you can see how Little Puddleton got its name. Although, if one looked into it properly, it would probably turn out to be some Anglo-Saxon derivative that had nothing to do with the state of the roads at all."

I deposited the plate in front of Toy Boy and shook my head at him when he moved to pass it on. The buck—the plate—stopped there. He looked down at it as though he would not mind if it didn't stop at all.

"I'm glad it isn't steak," he murmured as he noticed me watching him.

"Why? Are you a vegetarian?" There was an indeterminate sort of meat in the casserole, but not much, from the look of it. Or perhaps Aunt Maddy had deliberately seen to it that the plate intended for Toy Boy was mostly gravy. She had ways of making her displeasure felt.

"No, I've just got a good sense of self-preservation,"

he said. "I wouldn't trust that old bat if there were steak knives around. I'd have one between my shoulder-blades the minute I turned my back on her."

"Then don't turn your back on her," I said sharply. "It's not polite, anyway."

"And *she's* been so polite to me!"

"If you think you're having a hard time with Aunt Maddy, wait until Uncle Wilmer arrives."

"Oh, I know all about *him*." Toy Boy looked grim. "We've already had one run-in."

"And that was just over taking his picture—" I couldn't resist it. "This time, you've taken his daughter."

"Taken her where?" He was indignant. "She's old enough to know her own mind. Hell, she's old enough to know everyone's mind!"

The last, carrying an assessment of Tamar's age, as well as the implication that she had made most of the running in their relationship—which none of us had doubted—fell into another of those unfortunate silences. This time, Tamar's glare was for him alone. It was as well that he had the room over the garage; it would be a lot more comfortable tonight than the floor would have been.

"Must be twenty minutes past the hour—" Ostentatiously, Jarvis Fortescue consulted his watch.

"Or twenty minutes to the hour—" Jennifer chimed in hastily.

"Well, it certainly isn't angels passing," Aunt Maddy said tartly. She filled the last plate and set it down firmly before her, looked around the picked up her knife and fork.

Mesmerized, we all followed suit, even Toy Boy, although he muttered something rebelliously.

"I beg your pardon?"

"The——" He cleared his throat and started again. "She's the old boy's sister, isn't she?"

"That's right," I said. "Why?"

"Runs in the family," he muttered. "She's barking mad, too."

"In that case," I said frigidly, "I'd be interested to know your real opinion of Tamar. She's also one of the family——"

There was a sudden outburst of barking. For a dizzy moment, I thought Toy Boy had erupted into a graphic demonstration of his opinion, then I realized that the dogs—who had been let out to run about the grounds while we dined—were giving simultaneous voice.

The doorbell began ringing. It rang and rang and rang, activated by a nerve-racked thumb, while the barking converged in the vicinity of the front door.

In the kitchen a dish crashed to the floor. Then another.

"I'll get it——" I stood up hastily. Aunt Maddy, who was having an attack of the *grande dames*, gave me a regal nod and turned to Godfrey, continuing a conversation which could not be heard above the barking.

I rushed to the front door and flung it open. A fugitive figure dashed past me for the sanctuary of the hallway. The dogs stopped barking abruptly.

In the silence Cromwell's challenging yowl rose to the skies: he would lick the stuffing out of any dog with guts enough to climb the tree and meet him nose to nose.

I slammed the door on them all and turned to face our unwary visitor. He was at the far end of the hallway, brushing himself off, smoothing his thin fair hair back and generally trying to reassert his personality after an unnerving experience.

"Good evening—" He gave me a tentative smile. "I'm, er, afraid I wasn't expected. I, er, I'm Ian Trifflin. Junior. You were expecting my father—but we're in partnership now and he's come down with influenza. He sent me here instead. He, er, he assured me that it would be all right—"

Outside, the barking recommenced and he winced. "I, er, I realize you were expecting me—him—us—tomorrow, but it was just as convenient for me to come down tonight—My father assured me that it wouldn't make any difference."

It wouldn't. Uncle Wilmer would be just as annoyed at being fobbed off with the Junior Triffid whether he arrived tonight or tomorrow. His father was obviously breaking him in to the partnership by throwing him in at the deep end. If Junior couldn't swim, the sooner they found out, the better.

"Have you eaten?" I asked. "We're just in the middle of dinner—"

"Oh yes, er, yes," he said quickly. "I stopped on the way down. That's why I'm late—why I wasn't earlier— One of the reasons—"

"All right." I cut him off before he launched into the story of his journey. There was a faint scene of strawberries in the air around him. He and Jarvis Fortescue could compare notes later.

"Perhaps you'd like to wait in the library," I said. "We won't be long. I'll have Mrs. Keyes—I'll bring you a drink myself. Brandy, perhaps?" He looked as though he could use something stiff and bracing.

"That would be fine." It was the first decisive statement I had heard him make so far. There was hope for the boy yet.

"This way." I led him into the library and darted into the drawing room, to return with the brandy decanter and a glass.

"We won't be long," I said truthfully, pouring a generous measure into the glass.

The hubbub outside was reaching epic proportions and his hand shook as he picked up the glass, trying not to glance towards the french windows.

"Excuse me a moment," I said in my most ladylike manner. I walked over to the french windows, while he flinched visibly, but I didn't open them. I simply stood there and bellowed, "*Shut up!*" It was the only way to deal with the dogs, but strangers didn't always understand.

"Aaah . . ." I don't know whether he understood or not, but he obviously appreciated the abrupt silence. Or perhaps it was just the brandy he appreciated. At any rate, he began to relax.

"I'm sorry," he said. "I'm not usually so nervous, but, er, my father didn't warn me that you kept a pack of Alsatians."

"We don't," I said. "They only sound like that." In the face of his obvious disbelief, I decided not to explain further. He could work it out for himself when he saw the menagerie later on.

"Dobermans, then—" He glanced anxiously towards the windows, obviously envisioning slavering monsters hurling themselves against the glass. "They can't get in, can they?"

"Not until we've finished eating," I said. My answer did not appear to soothe him.

"I, er, I left my cases in the car—" The glance he sent towards the french windows told me plainly that he was not going to go out there and get them by himself. I noticed, however, that he clung firmly to his briefcase. It was probably some sort of reflex action.

"Finish your drink," I said resignedly. "I'll get your cases and show you to your room."

"Oh, but I don't want to interrupt—I mean, you're in the middle of your meal—"

"It's all right." On my way through the kitchen earlier, I had observed prunes soaking. I had a pretty good idea of what Mrs. Keyes planned to foist on us for dessert. "I've finished eating."

CHAPTER 5

I KNEW IT WAS RAINING IN THE MORNING BEFORE I HAD even unwrapped the pillow from around my ears. The weekend had lacked only that.

I wiped drops of moisture from my face and opened one eye. I closed it again hastily.

I don't know why the expression is 'mad as a wet hen' when clearly, the creature most furious about getting wet is a cat.

"Mrr-yahh!" Cromwell spat and shook himself again—all over me.

"It's not my fault," I protested feebly. "Believe me, I had nothing to do with it."

"Mrr-yahh!" He didn't believe me. His baleful glare told me that I was personally responsible for every outrage this weekend had so far produced; from the influx of hated canines to the nearly as odious invasion of noisy humans—many of them strangers. And now, the final indignity: a soaking, drenching downpour which had dislodged him from his treetop retreat and meant that he was forced to seek refuge under the very roof sheltering his deadly enemies. It was more than any self-respecting feline should have to bear—and someone was going to pay dearly for it.

"Mrr-yahh!" he snarled again. He turned himself broadside to me and gave another vigorous shake. A shower of water splattered all over me. I was now nearly as wet as he was. I was also getting just as annoyed.

"Now look—" I said threateningly. I struggled up on one elbow and returned his baleful glare. "I had nothing to do with it, so you can stop knocking *me* about. I'm not one of your ruins—not yet!"

There was a good chance that I'd be a ruin by the end of the day, though, if I had to spend it cooped up in this house with all its disparate temporary occupants.

"Mrr-yrr-rr . . ." Grumbling to himself, Cromwell marched to the foot of the bed, stamping his feet all the way. He plumped himself down heavily, a damp patch spreading out around him, and arched his neck to try to wash the back of his neck.

"You won't get very far that way." I gave up, got up,

and went to fetch a towel. Cromwell must have crouched in the tree, defying the rain, for as long as he could possibly stand it. He was drenched.

Still protesting, Cromwell allowed me to wrap him in the towel and begin blotting him dry. There was an air of secret relief about him; he had obviously begun to suspect that it might be a bigger job than one tiny pink tongue could manage.

"There now," I said. "Isn't that better?" He was still looking half-drowned, but most of the excess water had been absorbed by the towel.

"Come downstairs, now," I told him. "Someone will have switched on the fire in the drawing room and you can lie in front of it and dry out." I would also get him a saucer of milk with a dollop of brandy in it to ward off pneumonia. Nothing would upset Uncle Wilmer more than to find Cromwell ailing. He would claim that we had not taken proper care of his beloved pet. It would get his homecoming off on the wrong foot. Apart from which, I was quite fond of Cromwell myself.

"Come on." Still cuddling him in the towel, I carried him downstairs. He stretched up and rubbed his head against my chin, leaving a wet streak, then settled in my arms purring. This was more like it; this was where he belonged—not driven up on to an uncomfortable bough by the presence of the hated enemy.

Somewhere in the house, one of the dogs began barking. Cromwell tensed instantly and issued a loud yowling challenge.

"Okay, okay, take it easy." I shook him gently. "I won't let them bother you."

I wouldn't. I felt violently partisan. This was Cromwell's

home, the others were just visiting. It was unfortunate that the downpour would prevent the dogs being turned loose in the grounds, as they had been last night, but there were other options. If they get too obstreperous, they could be banished to the garage—or the room over it.

Let Toy Boy work his passage by keeping them under control. It was a solution I knew Aunt Maddy would unhesitatingly endorse. And, after all, he was already well-versed in taking care of Frou-Frou. He might not find it so difficult to handle them.

Meanwhile, I gained the drawing room and found—as I might have expected—that no one had done anything in there yet. The dank chill struck to the marrow of my bones and Cromwell muttered uneasily.

"Relax, it won't take long." I set him down in a corner of the sofa and turned to switch on the electric fire. Above the hearth, the portrait of Aunt Nora smiled down on me approvingly.

It took a few minutes before the fire began to warm up. Cromwell settled into a half-doze, exhausted by his long vigil on the bough. I switched on the radio. We were close enough to London to bring in LBC and I was just in time to catch the traffic report. I listened while Scotland Yard and the Automobile Association brought listeners up to the minute on the state of the roads and motorways. Then it was time for the air traffic reports and I was unnerved to learn that favorable tailwinds over the Atlantic during the night meant that most flights from the United States would be arriving an hour or so ahead of schedule.

It was just as well that Uncle Wilmer had insisted that

we were not to bother meeting him. It was one thing if his plane were late and we had been hanging around for several hours—it would be quite another thing if he arrived early and, unforgivably, no one was there to greet him.

But this meant that he might be here for lunch, when we had not been expecting him before tea. For a panic-stricken moment, I felt like rushing through the house, banging on doors, trying to rouse everyone to meet this unexpected emergency.

Then I remembered that, however early the plane, it would still take time for passengers to clear Customs and Immigration. Not to mention transport into the center of London and then connecting with British Rail services to Little Puddleton.

As the saying went, what you lost on the swings, you gained on the roundabouts. Or, in this case, what Uncle Wilmer gained on the tailwinds, he'd lose on the timetables.

Cromwell gave a sudden plaintive little whimper and I was brought sharply back to the here-and-now. The future could take care of itself; Cromwell needed that brandy-fortified milk immediately.

I patted Cromwell soothingly and went out into the kitchen. Still, no one was stirring. I took a soup plate from the cupboard and retrieved the morning's milk delivery from the back doorstep. With no qualm of conscience at all, I liberally poured coffee cream into the soup plate instead of milk. If Mrs. Keyes wanted to know what had happened to her cream, I would cheerfully shift the blame to my cousins—or perhaps even Toy Boy. It was all in a good cause.

Cromwell opened one eye hopefully as I crossed through

the drawing room. He was ever alert to anything to his advantage.

"Just another minute," I assured him, opening the library door. I had last seen the brandy decanter in there, in the custody of the Junior Triffid.

Sure enough, it was on the desk, considerably depleted since that last sighting. I remembered that Godfrey had been muttering something about plying the Triffid with strong waters and trying to get advance information about Sir Wilmer's intentions. I wondered if he had had any success with his mission, but doubted it. My guess was that the Junior Triffid knew no more about anything than we did. Uncle Sir Wilmer would divulge his plans in his own good time.

In the meantime, Cromwell was sitting up and eyeing me hopefully. I set the bowl of cream down on the coffee table, which I pulled into its winter position in front of the sofa, away from the fire. He shook off the towel and lurched forward.

"Hold it." I held him back while I poured a dollop of brandy into the cream and stirred it with a forefinger. Then I stepped back, still clutching the brandy decanter and licking my finger while Cromwell launched himself into the nectar, purring loudly and appreciatively.

"Oh, er, pardon me—" I looked up to find the Junior Triffid standing in the doorway, his eyes fixed on the brandy decanter with horrified surmise. He obviously thought it was my breakfast.

"It's all right. Come in." Wickedly, I considered confirming all his worst suspicions by knocking back some brandy—perhaps even without bothering to use a glass—but it was far too early in the morning and I'm not too keen on brandy at the best of times. Resignedly, I replaced the decanter on the drinks trolley, but disdained to explain.

"I, er, I was beginning to think I was the only one awake." He moved cautiously into the room. "I wasn't sure what one did about—" Studiously, he averted his eyes from the brandy. "About breakfast."

Cromwell raised his head and gave him a baleful look. He halted in mid-step. He seemed to be an excessively timid young man. Was there no animal he was not afraid of?

"Have you ever met Uncle Wilmer?" The thought followed on naturally.

"Er, actually, no—" Not being able to follow my thought process, the question seemed to puzzle him.

"Wait until you beard the lion in his den, then." I bent to stroke Cromwell soothingly.

"Er, yes." This time he allowed his glance to rest briefly on the brandy decanter.

"About breakfast." He decided to try again, speaking slowly and distinctly. "Perhaps there's some place in the village where I could get a bite to eat? Perhaps you'd like to join me? We could have some coffee—" He added thoughtfully. "Black coffee."

"We have plenty of food in the house," I said coldly. "And the kitchen is this way..." I swept out of the room, carefully not looking back.

Tamar and Toy Boy were prowling around the kitchen. A pot of coffee was just beginning to bubble. Tamar was opening cupboard doors at random, while Toy Boy investigated the contents of the fridge. The apricot poodle whisked between one and the other, pausing only to yap sharply at the Triffid as we entered.

"Aunt Maddy seems to have gone on strike—" Tamar greeted us. "I don't suppose you know where Mrs. Keyes hides the cups these days?"

"She moved them to the cupboard under the sink at Spring Cleaning," I said. "But, if they aren't there, you might try the back of the pantry shelves." Mrs. Keyes had her own guerrilla warfare methods of proving she was indispensable. Her standard ploy was to move the daily necessities from place to place, so that she could demonstrate how invaluable she was, complaining all the while that no one could ever find anything without her assistance. Since she had hidden the objects in the first place, this was hardly surprising.

"She's getting worse—" Tamar unearthed the toaster from the breadbox and found half a loaf of bread in the flour canister. "Father is going to have to do something."

"Try to keep it cool over this weekend," I pleaded, retrieving cutlery from the biscuit box. "If Uncle Wilmer sacks her, she'll stay home for a week out of sheer spite."

The Triffid and Toy Boy had drawn together and were eyeing us as though we were speaking a foreign language.

"Aunt Maddy ought to keep better control—"

"Mrs. Keyes is better than no help at all!" It was all very well for Tamar to complain, she didn't have to live here. There weren't all that many women willing to "oblige" in this area. You took what you could get and were thankful—or moderately so. "At least she does the cleaning and cooking."

The cleaning was usually skimped and the cooking

was erratic, but there was no need to go into that. Uncle Wilmer had antagonized all previous—and more sensitive—"obligers" to the point where they had resigned. Fortunately, Mrs. Keyes seemed to look upon him more as a sparring partner than an employer and, on that basis, was content to remain.

"What—" Toy Boy seemed to be adapting to the situation faster than the Triffid—"what is the coal-scuttle doing under the table? And why is it covered with a tea towel?"

"Aha!" Tamar swooped on it, snatching off the cloth. The scuttle had been lined with newspaper and filled with fresh ripe fruit.

"Peaches!" Tamar exulted, emerging from beneath the table with a large luscious peach in each hand. "Oh, lovely! I'm a fool for peaches!"

"Hhmmph!" We had not heard Aunt Maddy coming. She stood in the doorway now, her sharp look telling Tamar that it was more than peaches she was a fool for."

"Er . . . sorry . . ."

"Ooops . . . sorry" The Triffid and Toy Boy collided, stepping back out of Aunt Maddy's way as she advanced into the kitchen.

"You can put those peaches back, Tamar," Aunt Maddy ordered crisply. "Mrs. Keyes is doing Peach Fool for Sunday lunch and we'll need them for it."

Tamar replaced one peach and bit into the other defiantly. Although she had been operating on a reasonably adult level so far this morning, she was regressing to the stage of a rebellious teenager now that Aunt Maddy was in the room.

"Those haven't been washed yet." Aunt Maddy reacted

calmly to the insubordination. "Either wash that or peel it before you eat it. You don't know what germs may be on it." She crossed to the dishwasher to remove cups and saucers, a place so obvious we hadn't thought of looking there.

Tamar stuck her tongue out behind Aunt Maddy's back, thereby regressing several more years, but she moved reluctantly to the sink and washed her peach. Tamar always took great care of her health.

The toast popped up with the usual accompanying clatter and the Triffid jumped as though someone had shot at him. I wondered if he were on the verge of a nervous breakdown—or perhaps in the middle of one. If so, it was not kind of his father to despatch him to a place like this. Unless the old boy worked on the kill-or-cure principle. In this case, it looked as though kill would win out.

"You don't want anything to elaborate, do you?" Aunt Maddy hinted broadly, pouring coffee for us. "Mrs. Keyes will be here early to start cooking—and you know how upset she gets if she finds anyone in her kitchen."

"It isn't *her* kitchen," Tamar said sulkily, slumping into a chair at the table. "It's *ours*."

"You can dispute that point with her, if you're fool enough," Aunt Maddy said. "Just don't do it this weekend. I have quite enough to contend with."

Tamar's reply was mercifully muffled as she bit savagely into her peach; juice ran down her chin and Frou-Frou leaped up to lick at it.

"Really!" Aunt Maddy winced and turned her eyes away. She did not sit down, but hovered over us in a manner guaranteed to unnerve the males.

If she kept it up, the Triffid would have a permanent twitch. Even Toy Boy seemed to be cracking under the strain. Both of them perched gingerly on the edge of their chairs, obviously wishing they were elsewhere.

"What time are we expecting Flora and Reggie?" I asked, more as a diversion than because I wanted the information.

A stricken look passed between the Triffid and Toy Boy. *There are more of them* was the anguished message I intercepted. They appeared to be linking up in a sort of partnership against the common threat. I didn't think Tamar was going to be too happy about that when she noticed it.

"Any time now." Aunt Maddy spoke with grim relish. Flora and Reggie could be depended upon to endorse her opinions; she was looking forward to the arrival of reinforcements.

Tamar ostentatiously gave an uncaring shrug. The disapproval of one more aunt and uncle-by-marriage was not going to change anything in her life, far less the way she lived it.

"Er—" The Triffid hastily gulped down his coffee and rose. "I think I'll stroll down to the village," he said, ignoring the pelting rain outside. "And, er, pick up a newspaper."

"*The Times*, the *Telegraph* and the *Guardian* have already been delivered," Aunt Maddy said. "You'll find them in the library."

"Oh, er, yes." He was nonplussed for only a moment; he was learning. "But, er, not what I'm interested in this morning. Must have one of the tabloids. Er, an article about one of our clients. I must check." He was obviously willing to claim an interest in the Page 3 girls if it would get him out of this house for a while.

"Good idea." Toy Boy pushed back his chair. "I'll come with you. The heavies aren't my style, either."

Aunt Maddy sniffed. "Do as you please." She glanced at Tamar. "This is Liberty Hall!"

They fell over each other getting through the doorway. It was clear that they were going to dive into the pub as soon as it opened and we wouldn't see them again until lunch. If then.

"*Now* look what you've done!" Tamar raged at Aunt Maddy. "You've driven away our guests!"

"If that's all it took—" Aunt Maddy was only too willing to cross swords—"they can't have been very anxious to stay."

"Excuse me," I said firmly, pouring a second cup of coffee and retreating with it. "I think I'll join Cromwell."

CHAPTER 6

WITH THEIR USUAL SUPERB TIMING, REGGIE AND AUNT Flora got to the house just in time for elevenses. By then, Mrs. Keyes had arrived and driven Tamar and Aunt Maddy out of the kitchen, where she was now crashing cups and saucers together in noisy protest at having to prepare mid-morning coffee for so many people.

"*So* lovely to see you again—" Aunt Flora kissed cheeks while Reggie put the car into the garage. "And such a happy occasion. *Sir* Wilmer, how fitting. And how well deserved."

"Save it until Will arrives," Aunt Maddy advised drily. "He'll be ready for some praise and comfort after his flight. They say re-entry is very hard after one of these American lecture tours. It will take him a while to get adjusted again."

"Oh, but he shouldn't feel neglected with two birthday parties waiting to welcome him home." Aunt Flora tossed her coat and gloves down on top of a sleeping Cromwell, who did not appreciate the gesture. The coat began to heave and toss as he fought his way free. The gloves fell to the floor and I retrieved them.

"Oh dear, I'm afraid I didn't notice the cat," Aunt Flora said, as Cromwell's furious head emerged. "Is he all right?"

"Nothing damaged but his dignity," I assured her. With cats, that was quite enough.

"Mrr-yahh!" Cromwell spat at us and leaped to the floor. He prowled over and looked through the french windows to find the rain still pouring down, cutting off his favorite line of retreat. Muttering fiercely, he flattened his ears and crawled under the sofa. There was no peace anywhere for a cat these days.

A clatter at the door announced Mrs. Keyes. She carried in the tray, deposited it on the coffee table and straightened to announce, "Corned beef salad for lunch. That's quite enough, as I've all the fancy cooking to do for the buffet tomorrow. Not to mention tonight." She looked around belligerently, waiting for complaint. The only one in a mood to take her on was Cromwell. A low growl came from beneath the sofa.

"That will do, Mrs. Keyes," Aunt Maddy said ambiguously.

"It had better!" Mrs. Keyes stamped off, leaving silence behind her until she was safely out of earshot.

"Oh dear," Aunt Flora sighed. "It's going to be like that, is it? All weekend, do you suppose?"

"I'm afraid so." Aunt Maddy sighed in her turn, but there was a gloating edge to her voice. "You haven't heard the worst of it yet. And what Wilmer will say—"

"I'll hang this up for you, Aunt Flora." Since I already held the gloves, I picked up the coat and retreated. They could indulge in a better grade of scandal without me around to put a damper on the conversation. By lunch time, Aunt Flora would have come to terms with the situation and Aunt Maddy would be considerably mollified by a long session with a sympathetic ear.

Tamar clumped down the stairs as I was hanging up the coat. She had changed into dark green whipcord knickerbockers under a bright yellow slicker, worn with shocking pink wellies, and was obviously off to the pub to give the villagers a few more hours of innocent amusement. Frou-Frou, buckled into a Black Watch tartan raincoat, frisked at her heels.

"Your Aunt Flora has arrived," I informed her.

"Oh God!" She rolled her eyes heavenwards.

"And there's corned beef and salad for lunch." She might as well know all the worst.

"Then we'll have a Ploughman's at the pub. Don't let them keep anything for us," she added anxiously. "Cromwell can have my share."

She tiptoed past the drawing-room, but it wasn't her day. Reggie was just outside the front door as she opened it.

"My favorite niece!" He gave her a smacking kiss, then looked around guiltily in case Jennifer were nearby to have her feelings hurt. "And my favorite not-quite niece." He gave me a kiss as well.

"Your *only* not-quite niece," I corrected him. Aunt Flora was Uncle Wilmer's sister-in-law, Aunt Nora's only sibling. As such, she was aunt and Reggie was uncle to Godfrey, Jennifer and Tamar, but not to me, except by courtesy of an extended family. No one worried much over proper titles, however.

"I'll see you later—" Tamar patted him on the shoulder and skipped around him.

"You're not going out in this?" But she was gone.

"Flora's in with Aunt Maddy—" I gestured towards the drawing room. "I'll go and tell Godfrey and Jennifer you've arrived. I think they're upstairs." At least, their animals were, the occasional bark had informed me.

"Oh, don't bother them. There's no rush. We'll be together all weekend." He nodded several times in confirmation of his own remark and disappeared into the drawing room.

I found Godfrey and Jennifer, with their dogs, in the study on the top floor. It had obviously been intended as a nursery originally, but since we had all been beyond the nursery stage when Uncle Wilmer acquired the house, it had been transformed into a second study which had become mine by right of eminent domain. I had begun using it as a quiet place to do my homework when at school and everyone had become so accustomed to having me use it that no one had ever questioned my right to do so.

Now Godfrey sprawled on the divan in the corner, Jennifer was seated at my desk absently doodling on the scratch pad, and the two dogs crouched on the window seat, looking out at the rain with every bit as much indignation as Cromwell.

"Here you are." I bit down on indignation myself. By rights, they should have been in one of their own rooms on the floor below. I felt as though my territory were being invaded. It was not a pleasant feeling.

"Flora and Reggie have arrived."

"Hail, hail, the gang's all here," Jennifer chanted softly.

"Nevertheless, Father will be pleased to see them," Godfrey reproved.

"Will he?" Jennifer shrugged. "It wouldn't cheer *me* to have this motley collection hanging around waiting to drag me down to earth after a high-flying lecture tour. I should think it would put him in the worst possible mood. Especially Tamar and her little Playmate of the Month."

"Ah well," Godfrey said gravely. "We must expect Father to be in a rather sombre mood, anyway. After all, it *is* his seventieth birthday and he *is* taking it seriously. The guest list proves it. Just consider: his lawyer, his bank manager, and now his accountant. I think we can safely assume Reggie is here in a semi-professional capacity, not just as Aunt Flora's husband."

"It does seem to augur that Father is going to be sensible." Jennifer shaded in a patch on the pad of paper. I was close enough now to see that it was not aimless doodling as I had first thought. Jennifer had sketched a shopfront, Georgian bow-window style, surrounded by figures and sums. It seemed that Jennifer was making advance plans for the disposition of anticipated largesse.

"It's only prudent," Godfrey said. I realized that he, too, had been jotting down sums on a small notepad half-concealed in his hand. He returned to an old grievance. "He should have done it years ago."

"Hopefully, it's a long way from being too late." Jennifer gazed thoughtfully at her notes, sketched a pair of ornamental hitching-posts to flank the shop door and added a three figures sum to the column of figures marching down the side of the sketch.

Silently, I watched Jennifer re-total the column of figures. Aunt Maddy had warned them about counting chickens. The shadow of the ever-present Delilah next door could not be brushed aside so lightly. After a long and exhausting trip, the lovely Davina might beckon like an oasis to a parched traveler. And she, too, had had a long talk with Uncle Wilmer before he left home and now seemed to be making plans of her own. It was a safe bet those plans wouldn't include watching her hoped-for husband's fortune being shared out among his children before she even got her name on a joint checking account.

At the window, Nell Gwynn gave a sudden gladsome yip and began wagging her tail, looking downwards.

Automatically, Godfrey and Jennifer rose to their feet, as though assuming battle stations.

"It's all right. It's not Uncle Wilmer." I crossed to the window, pushed the dogs aside and looked down.

It was as I had thought. Little Lynette was at her window in the cottage next door. She had obviously decided to look out to see if Uncle Wilmer had arrived yet. Or perhaps she had been detailed to stand watch by her mother.

"It's only Lynette," I reassured the others, waving to the child. "Her room is opposite Uncle Wilmer's study. She's at the window, watching for him."

"Oh, really!" Jennifer slumped back into her chair with a judder of indignation. "I don't know why Father puts up with that sort of nonsense. He ought to have a study where he isn't overlooked."

"It's only Lynette," I said again. "Uncle Wilmer doesn't mind her. And he can look into her room quite as easily as she can look into his."

"That's right," Godfrey said thoughtfully, crossing to join me at the window. "Father is quite fond of the child, isn't he?" He patted Rex absently, staring down at Lynette.

Lynette was the strongest card in Davina's hand—and we all knew it. It was a mark of Uncle Will's favor that she was allowed to occupy a room facing his. If he had raised any objection, Davina would have moved her to another room instantly. But Uncle Wilmer seemed to enjoy the child's company—although at a far remove.

"Lynette is a very bright child." I felt obscurely compelled to defend her. "And she has a very sweet personality."

"Mmmm," Godfrey said, sounding slightly like Aunt Maddy. "No doubt." He looked across at Lynette, his face impassive.

She stopped waving abruptly, as though aware of an inexplicable disapproval. Her bright smile faded. After a frozen moment, she disappeared from view, like a wild animal startled—or frightened—by the sudden appearance of a predator in what had hitherto been safe territory.

"Mmmm," Godfrey said again. He turned away from the window. Rex whined uneasily and leaped down from the window seat to follow his master across the room.

"Someone ought to walk the dogs," Jennifer said pointedly. "They've been in all morning."

"All right." Godfrey capitulated without argument. He appeared to be thinking of something else.

"You could just let them out for a run in the garden," I suggested.

"No," Godfrey said. "I'll take them for a proper walk."

"You'll find Tamar and Toy Boy at the pub," I warned him. "Also the Triffid."

"I wish you'd use their proper names," Godfrey said, with a sudden flash of irritation. "You're old enough to behave like an adult and stop giving everyone ridiculous nicknames."

"I don't know their proper names." I realized it with surprise. "None of us were ever properly introduced."

"And if you had been, you probably weren't paying attention." Jennifer weighed in against me. "You really are *too* careless, Pippa. Godfrey's right, it's time you grew up and stopped acting like a child."

"I'm *not*—" I stopped. There was no point in arguing. *Child* was the operative word, but I wasn't the child they were annoyed about. They were simply taking it out on me because they couldn't reach Lynette.

"All right." I called their bluff. "Since you're both so grown up and pay so much attention, *you* tell *me* what their proper names are."

That stopped them cold. They locked glances, each waiting for the other to provide the answer. There was a moment of silence.

"Come along, Nell," Godfrey called to the spaniel still crouched on the window seat. "Walkies!"

"Tamar is *so* scatty." Jennifer began to spread the blame. "You may be right about her...friend. I can't remember hearing any name for him at all. But I'm quite sure Mr. Trifflin's son is named Ian."

"Junior," I said. "But he'll always be the Triffid to me. Yes, he *did* introduce himself, even though he was terrified out of his mind by the dogs."

"Terrified by the dogs?" It was an alien concept to Jennifer. "How could he be? There must be something wrong with the man." Abstractedly, she began lettering a sign above the shop front in Olde Englishe script. Reading upside down, I could decipher: THE POOCH PARLOR.

"That wouldn't surprise me," I said truthfully. I had reached the stage where nothing would surprise me. Not even the realization that my Cousin Jennifer secretly longed to give up her successful career and retreat into the peaceful backwater of dog-breeding and running a pet shop on the side. Or was it that her career was giving her up? She was in a volatile profession with ambitious young people crowding up behind her. Come to think of it, it had been quite a while since I had seen her name in any credits.

And what of Godfrey? He was in a managerial post in a not very go-ahead firm. Was the firm falling even farther behind, with the specter of redundances looming on the horizon? Godfrey might be glad to get out of the rat-race. Would he be going into partnership with Jennifer?

Or did he have separate plans of his own? What dream did the figures on the scratch pad he had slipped into his pocket represent?

The dogs were at his feet, tails wagging, eyes bright and hopeful, begging him to end this delay. Rex uttered a short, pleading bark and Godfrey capitulated. He might be able to resist Jennifer's dog, he could not resist his own.

"I think the rain is letting up," he said, in the face of evidence to the contrary streaming down outside. "Might as well take them as far as the pub and have a drink before lunch."

"Just don't stay until closing time," Jennifer warned him. "Father won't be happy if we aren't all here to greet him."

"I'll be back in good time." Godfrey gestured to the dogs and they followed him from the room.

"I just hope he is." Jennifer looked after her brother with a frown. "And Tamar, too," she added with less concern. "Although that doesn't matter so much. In fact, it might be better if she weren't here. It's *too* bad of her to bring that terrible creature of hers along to a private family party."

"He isn't very happy about it himself," I said truthfully. There were moments when I could feel sorry for Toy Boy. He could never have had any idea of what he was letting himself in for. Perhaps he had imagined the rest of the family was as liberated and permissive as Tamar. If so, he had certainly realized his mistake rapidly. The trouble was that he was stuck with it just the same—for the entire weekend.

"Who cares what he thinks?" Jennifer turned back to her notes and added another set of figures.

"Presumably Tamar does—"

"For the moment," Jennifer cut me off rudely. "That's the only consolation about Tamar's fancies. They don't last long. She'll tire of him, or he of her, and they'll break up eventually." Jennifer sighed deeply. "Then heaven knows what she'll land us with next!"

"You have to admit—" I tried to be fair—"this one isn't too bad."

"On form, no," Jennifer had to agree. "At least this one is fairly presentable. But—" she broke off and shook herself.

"But Uncle Wilmer still isn't going to be pleased," I finished for her.

"I refuse to think about it any more." Jennifer sounded rather like Aunt Maddy at that moment. "Whatever happens, Tamar has brought it on her own head. Father can't possibly blame us for anything she does. He knows what she's like."

That was whistling in the dark if I ever heard it. Uncle Wilmer could find reasons to blame anyone for anything. Anyone but himself.

"Anyway, there are more important things to worry about right now," Jennifer said. "Have you got any wrapping paper and silver or gold ribbon? Godfrey's left it to me to wrap his birthday present to father. He just brought it down in the paper bag the store used and, of course, it didn't occur to him to pick up any wrapping paper. He just doesn't think of these things. I wrapped my present before I left London. I never thought of bringing extra paper and ribbon along."

"I'll find some." I was just as glad of the excuse to get away. There was a bit left over from my own present, but it would make a better display if every present had different wrappings. Uncle Wilmer had a keen eye for such little touches. Although he might inveigh in his books about the waste involved in gift-wrapping parcels, he would not thank Godfrey quite so warmly for something presented in a sack bearing the name of the shop it came from. "Aunt Maddy has some supplies tucked away somewhere."

"Hurry," Jennifer glanced at her watch. "You know we can't depend on Father arriving after lunch. If it doesn't take too long to clear the customs formalities, he could be here any minute now."

"On the other hand—" I knew perfectly well that Uncle Wilmer, no matter how quickly he got away from Heathrow, might decide on the petty drama of a delayed arrival—"on the other hand, he might not get here for hours yet."

I had no idea how right I was.

CHAPTER 7

BY MID-AFTERNOON THE TENSION WAS BEGINNING TO tell. The rain had not let up. The pub was closed. Not that anyone would have dared to slope off to the pub with Sir Wilmer Creighleigh's arrival imminent. The house was in order; the preparations were finished. We had nothing to do but sit around and snap at each other.

Jarvis Fortescue had prudently withdrawn to his room, claiming that he must get on with some work he had brought down with him. He had also spent most of the morning in his room. Of course, he had been down here for weekends before. He always brought a briefcase along, explaining that the pressure of work necessitated it. We had no way of knowing whether the briefcase actually held work so important it could not wait until Monday, or simply contained the latest paperbacks. He wasn't a bank manager for nothing.

By late afternoon, we had even got beyond the point of snapping at each other. Perhaps Mrs. Keyes's corned beef salad was taking its toll. We had regrouped and were sitting around the room in silent pairs, abandoning any pretense at social conversation.

Even Cromwell had declared a temporary truce and was allowing Nell and Rex to share the hearthrug with him. Frou-Frou, he continued to keep at bay; she was too skittish for his liking. She had retreated to Tamar's lap, pretending that that was where she really wanted to be.

When the telephone rang, we all jumped. Aunt Maddy and I were sitting nearest and she beat me to it. A look of exasperation spread over her face as she listened to the voice at the other end of the line.

"No, Davina—" Aunt Maddy spoke with elaborate patience. "No, Wilmer hasn't arrived yet . . . Yes, he *is* later than we expected. . . . No, I don't think anything has happened . . . If it had, we'd have heard it on the five o'clock news bulletin . . ."

Or the police would have been at the door to notify the next-of-kin personally before releasing the news to the general public.

The unspoken thought was in every mind. You could see it flickering behind their eyes as every head turned instinctively towards the windows, as though expecting to see a tall, blue, helmeted figure at the front door.

"No . . . No, that's all right, Davina . . ." Aunt Maddy continued speaking with exaggerated restraint, but with a note in her voice that warned that she was about to bring the conversation to a close. "I quite understand. Naturally you were concerned. Of course you couldn't help but have noticed if he'd arrived—"

There were several suppressed smiles in the room. We all shared a mental picture of Davina poised behind the curtains, keeping watch for the return of the conquering hero.

"It's *still* six-thirty for dinner at seven—" Aunt Maddy spoke with mixed emotion. Pleas, veiled threats and proffered bribes had not swayed Mrs. Keyes: dinner should be served at six. In only the most exceptional circumstances was she willing to serve it later. Seven was as close to decadence as she was reluctantly prepared to go. Any later than that and we would have to serve ourselves.

"Of course he'll be here by then—" There were surreptitious glances at watches all around: it was quarter past five. "Don't be silly, Davina. We'll expect you and Lynette at six-thirty." Aunt Maddy replaced the receiver firmly.

"He probably had business in London," Aunt Flora said unconvincingly. "He's *sure* to be here any minute now—"

Davina arrived at six, unable to keep away any longer. "I'm sorry to be so early," she apologized, pushing

Lynette into the room ahead of her, "but I couldn't stay at home any longer, not knowing what was happening. He hasn't arrived?" She scanned the room, even though her vigil at her window had provided the answer.

"Not yet," Aunt Maddy said. Her smile was a trifle grim, but she did not quite dare to suggest that Davina should have waited for the proper hour. None of us quite knew what status Uncle Wilmer might have promised her upon his return.

"And no telephone call?" Davina was certainly anxious.

Aunt Maddy shook her head. "Put the presents on the table with the others, Lynnie," she directed.

Lynette hung her head and stayed close to her mother, overcome by shyness at the sight of so many strangers in the room. She clutched two gaily wrapped packages, one long and narrow, one of a less suggestible size.

"Surely Sir Wilmer would have telephoned if he'd missed his flight," Davina fretted. Even in her anxiety, she lingered gloatingly over the *Sir*. I refrained from looking at Aunt Maddy, but knew she would not have missed it. Yes, Davina was definitely taking a proprietorial interest in Uncle Will's new title. I'd be willing to bet that she'd been practicing "Lady Creighleigh" as her new title ever since the Honors List came out.

"Put the presents on the table, dear." Hand on shoulder, Davina urged her daughter forward, repeating Aunt Maddy's instruction. She stood over her as Lynette deposited the presents on the pile already heaped on the coffee table.

"No, like this, dear." Davina pulled their presents to the front and rearranged them to her own satisfaction. Stepping back, she allowed her gaze to drift up and across the portrait of Aunt Nora. A peculiar expression crossed her face, as though she were wondering why the painting was still in place; as though, in her own mind, it was already resting in the attic, face turned to the wall.

"Sit down, Davina," Aunt Maddy said. "You might as well have a drink. We all might as well."

"Right." Reggie had already started. He turned back to the drinks trolley, ready to act as barman. "Time for sundowners, anyway. Will has only himself to blame if he gets here and finds we're a couple of drinks ahead of him."

"Go with Pippa, Lynnie," Aunt Maddy said. "She'll get you a glass of milk or some orange juice."

Lynette followed me out to the kitchen, her self-confidence returning now that she was away from all the strangers.

"I got Uncle Will an umbrella," she boasted. "I picked it out myself. It has a parrot's head for a handle. My mother says it's an antique, but it's in good condition."

"That's fine," I said absently. It was to be hoped that Uncle Wilmer wouldn't take the gift personally. Before he left, he had shown signs of increasing touchiness at references to his age. It might have been more tactful to buy him something modern.

But that was Davina's problem. She might just get away with it since the card would be signed with Lynette's name. Her own present looked suspiciously like a book—always a dicey gift to someone who fancied himself a bibliophile. None of the family would be upset if her choice were so inept that Uncle Wilmer broke off diplomatic—and all other—relations.

"Not here yet, is he?" Mrs. Keyes greeted us with

grim relish. "Well, I've put the roast in the oven and if he isn't here when it comes out, that's up to him. We eat at seven—and that's all there is to it. I've a life of my own, you know, and my family expects me home at a decent hour."

"Quite right, Mrs. Keyes," I agreed cravenly, pushing Lynette forward. "But meanwhile, do you think you could find a glass of milk for Lynnie?"

"I'd rather have orange juice," Lynette said firmly.

"I'm afraid we don't have any," I said. "Perhaps Tamar finished it this morning. There wasn't any when I looked for it at breakfast-time."

It was touch-and-go for a moment, but Mrs. Keyes rose to the challenge. Lynette was a favorite, even with her.

"Bless her! Of course, she shall have orange juice if she wants it." Mrs. Keyes delved into the depths of the fridge. She pulled open the salad drawer and removed a plastic bottle labeled "Weed Killer."

"None of you can ever find anything!" She poured an orange stream triumphantly into a glass. "You'd never manage for ten minutes by yourselves without me." *What you really need is a keeper,* she implied.

I closed my eyes momentarily, feeling quite dizzy. It had never occurred to me to look in the salad drawer. I hadn't opened it since that day last summer when I had pulled it out to discover a mouse trap, complete with trapped mouse, keeping fresh for Cromwell's supper.

"I hope that bottle has been well-scrubbed." I spoke severely, trying to establish my authority. The attempt was foredoomed, as usual.

"As though I'd harm a hair of my little lamb's head,"

Mrs. Keyes said indignantly. "If your aunt hadn't taken all the glass bottles for her parsnip wine—which didn't even turn out well, I might add—I wouldn't be reduced to scrounging any old thing I can find for the necessities. I don't know—"

"Yes, I'm sure." I beat a hasty retreat, leaving Lynette in the kitchen. She was better able to cope with Mrs. Keyes than I was. Furthermore, she couldn't read awfully well yet and what she didn't know wouldn't hurt her.

In the hallway I encountered Tamar making for the front door, Toy Boy, Triffid and Jarvis Fortescue in her wake.

"Don't try to stop me," she said. "It's too stuffy to bear in there. I can't stand it for another minute. And—" she indicated her entourage—"neither can they."

"But Uncle Wilmer is sure to arrive the minute you've gone." I protested. "He's way overdue now."

"That's just it. I don't believe he's coming!" Tamar faced me defiantly. "If you want to know what I think, I think he's probably collapsed at Kennedy Airport before boarding the plane. They've probably got him in some Intensive Care Unit right now, fighting for his life—"

"Surely we'd have heard," I said. "Someone would have notified us."

"Why? There's nothing we can do at this distance. We couldn't even get there in time to say goodbye. They're probably working over him and waiting until they can tell us the worst is over and he's resting comfortably, or else that he's . . . gone."

Behind her, the men shuffled their feet uneasily. The Triffid, as the legal expert among them, took a short step forward. "I, er, I don't really think they'd do that," he said. "Of course, it might be that they had difficulty in trying to get through to the family. Er, all the telephone lines engaged, or something . . ." he tailed off unhappily.

"Perhaps he collapsed someplace else—" Tamar would not be diverted from her grim scenario. "He might have been mugged and all his identification stolen along with his wallet. He's in hospital, unconscious, and they have no way of knowing who he is, or who to notify. *And*," she added gloomily, "when they *do* find out and we get all those terrifying American hospital bills, it will probably eat up every penny of his money. There won't be anything left for any of us to inherit!"

"They couldn't be that bad." That was a point on which I could put her mind at rest. "In any case, I took out the maximum insurance on him. He's so well covered, there's no way the estate could be billed for an extra penny—even if the absolute worst happened and he lingered for months at maximum charges in a private room."

"Oh, well done, Pippa!" Tamar was momentarily cheered.

"But I don't believe for a moment that there's anything actually wrong," I went on. "And I think it's very silly of you to disappear now. You know he's bound to arrive as soon as you're out of sight."

"I suppose so, but I really can't stand it any longer in there with all of them sniping at me. We'll just walk as far as the pub, have a quick drink, and be back in time for dinner. If he comes, you can say Jarvis wanted to see the pub and dragged me along with him. Not even Father will argue with his bank manager—" She flashed a brilliant smile at Jarvis Fortescue. "You won't mind, will you, angel?"

Hysterical barking broke out behind the closed door of the drawing room. Frou-Frou had sensed that her mistress was about to depart without her and was making her sentiments known. The other dogs joined in. If anyone in the house was going out for a walk, it was their prerogative to be taken along.

"Oh, I can't—" As usual, Tamar evaded responsibility. "It's *too* much. We'll only be gone a few minutes. Quiet them, Pippa, won't you? There's a good girl." She slipped through the front door and was gone before I could protest. The others followed her swiftly.

Behind the door, the barking rose to hysterical pitch. The shouts of Godfrey and Jennifer also rose in volume as they tried to silence their own dogs.

If I opened the door now, the bedlam would escape into the hall. I could not face it. I turned and darted silently up the stairs. A few minutes of peace in my own room might restore me sufficiently to face the rigors of a family meal with the guest of honor conspicuously absent.

I curled up on the window seat overlooking the front drive. Thus I was in a position to see the hired car turn in at the gate before anyone else was aware of it. I left my perch and flew down the stairs in time to warn the others and be at the front door with Aunt Maddy in time to open it before Uncle Wilmer could ring the bell.

"Maddy—Pippa—" Uncle Wilmer embraced us. He had left the door open and, over his shoulder, I could see the chauffeur unloading suitcases from the car. There seemed to be a great many more than Uncle Wilmer had started out with. He must have gone on a shopping spree at every stop along the lecture circuit. I only hoped the presents we had waiting for him were opulent enough to match the ones he had brought us.

"Jennifer—Godfrey—" He moved beyond us to embrace his children. Abruptly, his affability was suspended as he sensed defection. He looked around the hall incredulously. "Where's Tamar?"

The happy babble of greetings silenced. Exchanged glances led Uncle Wilmer to expect the worst. When the silence had lengthened unendurably, it was left to me to break it.

"She'll be back any moment now," I said. "She's just gone down to the pub with Toy Boy."

"Toy?" Uncle Wilmer's voice rose nearly as high as his eyebrows. "Toy Boy? She's taken up with a Chinaman?"

"Come and sit down, Wilmer." Aunt Maddy caught at his elbow, pulling him into the drawing room. "You must be tired after your journey—"

"Wilmer!" Davina was waiting, posed dramatically beneath the portrait of Uncle Will's first wife. She swept forward to greet him, dipping in a half-curtsey. "*Sir* Wilmer," she breathed. "We are all so proud of you and so happy for you. *So* proud . . . *Sir* Wilmer."

For once, Uncle Wilmer was stopped in his tracks.

"Yes, yes—" He sounded oddly flustered. He backed away from her outstretched arms, stumbling into Aunt Maddy as he did so.

The dogs advanced upon him, yelping wildly, as though they had just discovered a burglar sneaking into the premises.

"Uncle Will! Uncle Will!" Lynette came pelting into the room to twine herself around him.

"You're looking a bit strained, Wilmer," Aunt Flora observed, not without a certain malice. "Was it a difficult flight?"

"Pay no attention to her, Will." Uncle Reggie came forward. "You're looking great. The tour's obviously done you a world of good."

"But what took you so long to get here, Sir Wilmer?" Davina captured his arm and led him to the sofa. "Was the flight delayed? Was there a bomb scare?" She sank down on the sofa and tried to draw him down beside her, but he remained upright, struggling to free his arm.

I heard thumping and bumping in the hall and went out to tell the chauffeur he might as well take the cases straight upstairs to Uncle Wilmer's room. It would save any of us having to do it later.

There was a pile of cases at the foot of the stairs and the front door was wide open. The chauffeur had obviously gone out to bring in the rest of the cases. How many more had Uncle Wilmer collected on his travels? No wonder he was so late; Customs must have had a word or two to say about all that shopping. Especially if he'd tried to go through the green Nothing to Declare lane. I hoped we weren't going to be treated to more newspaper headlines in the morning.

"He's here!" Tamar was back. She rushed through the doorway, the others following at a more sedate pace. "What kind of a mood is he in?"

"He noticed immediately that you were missing, if that's what you mean."

"Oh God! I'd better go in and face the music. Not you—" She put out her hand, stopping Toy Boy. "You wait here until I come for you."

The others seemed only too willing to obey the instruction as well, but I wouldn't let them. "You can go ahead in," I told Jarvis Fortescue and the Triffid. They might serve to deflect some of the attention from Tamar. Reluctantly they did so.

I waited on for the chauffeur. He seemed to be taking his time. Toy Boy cleared his throat a couple of times but seemed to be unable to think of anything to say. Then he made an extremely odd noise and I turned to look at him. He was staring over my shoulder, a strange expression on his face.

I whirled around. A pretty little waif who appeared to be in her early teens stood in the doorway, carrying two cases nearly as big as she was. There was the revving of an engine outside and the hire car drove away.

I blinked at her. She was obviously here to stay, but who was she? From the cut of her clothes and the style of her hair, I vaguely recognized that she must be American.

"Hi, there—" she said in the soft accents of the Southern states of America. "You must be Pippa." She set down her cases and held out her hand. "I'm Wanda-Lu. I sure do hope we're gonna be good friends."

I was conscious that Toy Boy had stretched out his hand and caught me gently under the chin, closing my mouth. It took an effort of will to clench my jaw and keep it closed.

"Now *that's* what I call a souvenir!" Toy Boy murmured in my ear.

"How do you do?" Dazedly I shook the outstretched hand, a dozen questions crowding my mind at the same time. I tried to sort them out into some form of order and tact. She must be the daughter of friends Uncle Wilmer had met on his tour. He had obviously invited her to use our house as a base—or perhaps even stay with us—while she made her tour of England. Without warning any of us in advance. Typical. Aunt Maddy was not going to be best pleased. The house was full. Even the room over the garage was taken. We would have to put her up somewhere in the village—

"Ah, there you are, my dear." Uncle Wilmer appeared in the doorway. "Come in and meet your new family." He led her into the drawing room. Mesmerized, Toy Boy and I followed behind.

"Maddy—Flora—Everyone—" Uncle Wilmer beamed impartially around the room. "I want you all to meet a very special person. I know you're going to love her as much as I do—"

I couldn't believe what I was hearing. Uncle Wilmer had obviously absorbed too many of those fulsome American introductions; they had turned his brain. In the ordinary way, he would never dream of talking like that. In fact, I had never before heard him admit that anyone else was in any way special. But he was still continuing, slowing a bit as he came to the crux of his introduction:

"Meet Lady Creighleigh . . . my wife."

CHAPTER 8

IT WAS JUST AS WELL THAT DAVINA WAS SITTING DOWN. She slumped back and closed her eyes. I couldn't tell whether she had fainted or not.

Jennifer began laughing senselessly again.

"You can't mean it," Aunt Maddy said faintly. "It's a joke. In very poor taste."

"See here—" Godfrey sputtered. "See here—" He was able to go no farther.

"I don't believe it," Tamar said flatly. "It isn't possible."

"I assure you," Uncle Wilmer said stiffly, "it's both possible—and legal. We were married two weeks ago in Maryland—in preference to Las Vegas. Wanda-Lu is my bride, my lawful wedded wife. And—" he added wickedly—"I think you ought to be more polite to your new mother."

"Mother!" Tamar was agonized. "That's ridiculous! She's younger than we are. She's even younger than Pippa!"

"How old is she?" Aunt Flora spoke in frozen, forbidding tones. "Exactly?"

"I'm seventeen," Wanda-Lu answered defiantly. "Seventeen and a half, if you want to be exact. And I'm old enough to know my own mind."

"How could you?" Godfrey faced his father indignantly.

"I told you they were gonna be kinda upset, Wilmer." Wanda-Lu was apparently given to massive understatement. "I told you we shouldn't 'a bothered."

"Don't distress yourself, my dear," Uncle Wilmer said unnecessarily. Wanda-Lu was the least distressed person in the room.

Even the dogs had begun whimpering restively, sensing the emotional storm engulfing their humans. Any moment now they would begin barking and have to be let out.

Cromwell gave them a look of cold contempt. He rose, stretched, and sauntered forward, leaping up on the coffee table to greet Uncle Wilmer.

"Ah, there's the nicest present of them all." Uncle Wilmer bent to stroke him. "Did you miss me while I was away, Cromwell?"

"Oh, Cromwell! I've heard all about you—" Wanda-Lu greeted him with more enthusiasm than she had greeted the rest of us. "And I've brought you a lovely catnip mouse! Now what do you think of that?"

Cromwell appeared to be considering the question. Then he arched his neck and rubbed his head against Wanda-Lu's outstretched hand. Trust Cromwell.

Tamar gasped in indignation and Frou-Frou immediately began barking as though in protest at Cromwell's defection to the enemy. The other dogs joined in and there was uproar.

Davina remained silent and motionless on the sofa, eyes still closed. Perhaps she really had fainted. Lynette huddled, wide-eyed, at her side.

"Out! Out!" Aunt Maddy opened the french windows

and made a sweeping gesture at the dogs. "Out—all of you!"

By this time, Cromwell was nestled in Wanda-Lu's arms. He looked down at the dogs smugly. When Aunt Maddy closed the windows behind the dogs, the loudest sound in the room was his purr.

"May I offer my congratulations, Sir Wilmer?" Smoothly, Jarvis Fortescue stepped forward to remind the family that there were strangers in their midst and to deflect further indiscretions. "On your marriage, on your knighthood, and on your birthday. This is indeed a happy—" he caught Aunt Flora's poisonous glare and faltered momentarily—"a happy occasion."

"Thank you, Fortescue." Uncle Wilmer was close to purring himself. "Very kind of you. And—" he added fiercely—"very civilized."

"It's all so sudden." I spoke weakly, as no one else seemed about to say something. "It will take some getting used to. But I'm—*we're*—very happy for you, Uncle Will . . . Uncle *Sir* Wilmer."

"Thank you, Pippa." Uncle Wilmer beamed at me. "I'm sure *you* will adjust rapidly to the situation. I expect you and Wanda-Lu to become good friends." It was an order.

"I'm sure we will." I smiled feebly at Wanda-Lu. Lady Creighleigh. She seemed a nice enough child, but she was certainly going to be out of her depth in this family. There were moments when even I felt as though I were going down for the third time—and I had been born into it."

"Er, yes, congratulations—" The Triffid stumbled forward, ever ready to follow a good lead. "Congratulations,

Sir Wilmer. And, er—'' he turned to Wanda-Lu—''the, er... very best wishes.'' It sounded as though he had just stopped himself from saying, *The best of British luck*.

''Why, thank you, Mr.—?'' She widened her eyes, turning from one to the other. ''I'm sorry. Wilmer isn't terribly good at introductions.''

''Fortescue, my—*our*—bank manager.'' Uncle Wilmer indicated the older man brusquely. ''And I'm afraid I'm not sure—?''

''Ian Trifflin—'' the Triffid put in hastily. ''Your, er, your solicitor's son. I've gone into the firm now.''

''Where's your father?'' Uncle Wilmer demanded, as though he were being fobbed off with an inferior reproduction.

''At home. He's, er, in bed, with ''flu.''

''At this time of the year?''

''It can strike at any time.'' Ian Trifflin defended his father against the unfair attack. ''It may be worse some seasons of the year, but there's no, er, exclusive season for ''flu.''

Uncle Wilmer grunted disbelievingly, but was distracted by catching sight of Toy Boy. ''*Who*—'' he demanded—''are *you*?''

''His name is Danny Lora.'' Tamar came forward. ''He's *my* friend.''

''Oh?'' Uncle Wilmer frowned at Toy Boy. In other circumstances, he might have launched into a juicy scene, but right now he was in no position to call the kettle black. ''You look vaguely familiar—'' he temporized. ''Have we met before?''

''Not officially,' Toy Boy said. ''We saw each other at Heathrow a couple of months ago. When you smash—''

He broke off abruptly as Tamar kicked him. I could see her point. This was not a moment for aiding old grievances. There were too many new grievances in the air.

"Pardon me." A voice spoke from the doorway. We turned. It was all we needed. Mrs. Keyes, scenting drama from afar, had hurried to find out what was going on. She stood in the doorway, eyes alight, taking in the scene.

"Dinner will be ready in ten minutes, Sir Wilmer." She had never bothered to be so formal before. "But if you're not ready yet, I can easily put it back for an hour or so. It doesn't matter—" she simpered ingratiatingly— "if I go home a bit late. After all, you don't get back from America every day. My family will understand."

Translation: It was going to take dynamite to blast her out of the house tonight.

I exchanged glances with Aunt Maddy. Mrs. Keyes's family would understand all right, when she swept in loaded with gossip and scandal and first-hand reports on how we were taking the unexpected advent of a teen-aged Lady Creighleigh. She was probably already planning how much she could get from a Sunday scandal sheet for her revelations.

"Thank you, Mrs. Keyes." Uncle Wilmer was straight-faced, although he knew her as well as we did. "That's very obliging of you indeed. We could use an extra half-hour to freshen up. We've had a long journey."

"We surely did have," Wanda-Lu said. "Even when we got down on the ground, we came the long way around. Wilmer wanted to show me all his favorite places along the way."

"So that's why you were so late," Aunt Maddy said. "You might have let us know."

"We wanted to surprise you," Uncle Wilmer said.

Aunt Maddy's sniff told him that he had succeeded—and then some.

"And now I must take Wanda-Lu on a tour of the house," Uncle Wilmer said fondly. "I'm afraid it's a bit too wet for the garden right now. That will have to wait for tomorrow morning."

"Tomorrow . . . and tomorrow . . . and tomorrow . . ." It was impossible to tell who had whispered it. Someone who had begun to realize what Wanda-Lu's presence entailed. No lips had seemed to move, no eyes had met. Perhaps I hadn't heard the words at all; perhaps they existed only in my own mind. Or perhaps they had sprung simultaneously into everyone's mind, with such force that they had seemed to take audible form.

Instinctively I glanced at Davina. She still had not stirred. Her face was ashen.

Heaven knows, we had laughed enough in the past at her open pursuit of Uncle Wilmer, but it had abruptly ceased to be funny. At one stroke, she had lost more than Jennifer, Tamar and Godfrey. They, at least, still had their careers and their flats in London. Whereas Davina had retreated to Little Puddleton after her divorce, using her settlement as down payment on the cottage and saddling herself with an uncomfortably stiff mortgage.

If her gamble had paid off and she had captured Uncle Wilmer, all her financial problems would have been solved. Now she was stuck with the cottage, an expensive distance from London, in a village notably short of eligible males. Furthermore, she had now lost what dubious status she had had as Uncle Wilmer's unofficial companion. Local hostesses would no longer invite Davina

to parties in order to "make a pair" when they invited
Sir Wilmer. Quite the contrary. She was now someone
who could not safely be invited to social occasions
graced by the new Lady Creighleigh. She was a potential
embarrassment, if not a pariah.

"Shall I bring a cup of tea for Mrs. Hardy?" Mrs.
Keyes spoke with ill-concealed relish. "She does look
poorly."

Her remarks fell into the silence. For the first time,
Uncle Wilmer looked discomfited.

"That's an excellent idea, Mrs. Keyes. Please see to
it." Aunt Maddy took instant revenge. "In fact, as we
won't be dining for some while yet, you might bring tea
for all of us." We didn't want it and we wouldn't drink
it, but it had put Mrs. Keyes firmly back in her place.

"Very good, madam." Mrs. Keyes withdrew sulkily,
with more work than she had bargained for, but obviously still determined to play out her self-appointed role of
faithful family retainer in front of this new audience.

"Come along, Wanda-Lu," Uncle Wilmer said. "We'll
go up to my—*our*—room and—" He broke off as Davina
opened her eyes and looked at him accusingly.

"Pippa, I'll go through my notes after dinner—" He
turned to me, escaping into business matters. "See what
we've got." He frowned portentously. "I still haven't got
a title I'm happy with. We'll have to work on it. I want
to keep to the *Fool* theme. It's gone down especially well
in the States—"

Davina had closed her eyes again. She was still motionless, that was the only sign of life she had given.

"Come along, Wanda-Lu," Uncle Wilmer led the way
from the room hastily, before Davina could recover

enough to find her voice. He hurried his bride from the room.

"If you'll excuse me—" Jarvis Fortescue was evidently well-practiced in strategic withdrawals. "I find I've left some rather important papers in my room. I must consult them—" Murmuring discreetly and flashing a meaning glance at the two other non-family members in the room, he slipped out of the door.

"Yes. Er, yes." The Triffid stumbled towards the door. "Me, er, too. This changes . . . puts a different complexion on . . . er . . . I want to telephone my father and have a word . . ." He disappeared in Jarvis Fortescue's wake.

Toy Boy remained rooted to his spot. He was made of sterner—or brassier—stuff than the other two. He seemed only to be regretting that he hadn't his camera with him.

Davina lay motionless, mute and miserable. Uneasily I crossed to her side. "Davina," I said, "are you all right?"

"I don't believe it," she whispered. "I can't!" Her eyes opened slowly. "He promised me—" She raised her hand to press her fingertips against her lips, as though cutting off further indiscretions.

"Wanda-Lu . . ." Jennifer said reflectively. "How long do you suppose it will take some snappy headline writer to come up with *Wanda-Lust*?"

Toy Boy's eyes gleamed and I knew what the first pictures he sneaked away would be captioned.

"Don't you dare!" Tamar caught it too, and advanced upon him threateningly. He pantomimed improbable innocence and a complete unawareness of what she could possibly mean.

"A title!" Aunt Maddy said explosively. "I'll give him his next title: *No Fool Like an Old Fool!*"

CHAPTER 9

"WHEN YOU *THINK*..." AUNT FLORA SPOKE BETWEEN clenched teeth to the indignation meeting convened in the library next morning. "Just *think* of all the men—some of them a lot younger than Wilmer—who have had *flings* with young girls and never survived the exertion! There are cases in the newspapers all the time. *Those* men don't get up and go on to marry the girl and bring her home to embarrass their family. *They* expire...in the act!"

She made it sound as though it were the decent thing to do. Rough on the girl, perhaps, but showing a fine sensibility on the gentleman's part.

"The Creighleighs were always a very robust family," Aunt Maddy said, not without a trace of pride.

"Look on the bright side," Uncle Reggie said cheerfully. "Something might happen to the girl. Might even get hit by a car. We drive on the wrong side of the road over here, so far as she's concerned. If she were to go for a walk down one of the narrow lanes without paying enough attention..."

"That is too far-fetched," Aunt Flora said decisively. But there had been a thoughtful pause first.

"It would never do." Aunt Maddy had also noticed the pause. "We must take good care of her, or Wilmer would never forgive us."

"At this point," Aunt Flora said coldly, "I am not particularly worried about Wilmer's reactions. He appears to have taken leave of his senses—"

"Of everything *but* his senses, I'd say," Godfrey muttered.

"—and must be treated accordingly," Aunt Flora continued smoothly. "There's no need to be coarse, Godfrey. We'll get quite enough of that from the newspapers as soon as they learn about it."

Tamar moaned softly.

"Well, we must face up to it," Aunt Flora said briskly. "They'll make a Roman holiday of it. Wilmer was a media celebrity even before he was knighted. And now he's just had his seventieth birthday *and* brought home a seventeen-year-old bride. I can only be thankful my poor dear sister never lived to see this day!"

"If Nora were still alive," Aunt Maddy pointed out tartly, "this day would never have arrived. At least," she added thoughtfully, "I hope not."

"Oh, this is frightful!" Tamar said. "It's disgraceful! It's—it's *unseemly*!"

Coming from Tamar, that was rich. Even richer was the sight of Tamar and her aunts united in indignation over a moral issue. But, somehow, I didn't feel like laughing.

"What's that—?" Aunt Maddy gasped.

We followed her gaze and saw the doorknob noiselessly turning. Deep silence fell over the library. Like conspirators, we held our collective breath and watched the doorknob slowly return to its original position. there was no sound on the other side of the locked door.

We waited, but there was no knock upon the door. The person on the outside was not about to insist upon right of entry. After long frozen moments, we realized that whoever it was had silently gone away.

"Where are they?" Aunt Flora was almost whispering. There could be no doubt who she meant by *they*.

"*They've* gone for a drive through the countryside," Aunt Maddy said. "It must have been one of the houseguests."

"Are they still here?" Jennifer gave a low, wild laugh. I couldn't blame her.

During the awkward, but mercifully rushed, dinner last night, Jarvis Fortescue had been grave and abstracted, giving every indication of a man about to receive an urgent summons requiring his presence elsewhere—just as soon as he could gain access to a private telephone and arrange for it.

The Triffid had returned from his conversation with his 'flu-bedded father in somewhat more cheerful mood, but with an added nervous twitch of suddenly looking through the nearest window and scanning the horizon, as though he expected to see John Wayne leading the cavalry to the rescue of the beleaguered fort.

Only Toy Boy had shown no signs of wishing to be elsewhere—this was where the action was. He did appear to be regretting the absence of his camera. He could not have been the one who had just tried to enter the library. It was dollars to doughnuts that he had screwed his telephoto lens on to his new camera and was out stalking his prey right now.

None of them had shown up for breakfast this morning. It was hardly surprising. They wouldn't have wanted to risk facing a repetition of last night's awkwardness. Quite probably, their digestions hadn't recovered yet.

As it happened, they needn't have worried. Uncle Wilmer and Wanda-Lu hadn't come down to breakfast, either.

Not that that had made for a peaceful meal. If there was one thing more calculated to disturb the family than the presence of bright and shining bridal faces at the breakfast table, it was their absence. The family had had to sit around the table, choking down coffee and brioche all they could face—along with the knowledge that the newlyweds were still upstairs . . . in bed . . . together.

"Oh, it's monstrous!" Tamar raged. "How could Father *do* such a thing? The whole family will be a laughingstock!"

"I might say, Tamar—" Godfrey's tone reminded her that she was in no position to start throwing rocks; the circumstances of her last divorce—when her husband and current lover had battled through the expensive flat she had been hired to decorate—had been widely and hilariously reported—"I might say you haven't helped matters any. Bringing a press photographer down here this weekend."

"How was I supposed to know that Father had gone mad in America?" Tamar countered wildly. "How could any of us have imagined that he was going to bring home a child bride? A child," she wailed. "She's even younger than Pippa!"

"I'm not *that* young!" I was getting a bit fed up with Tamar's insistence on my youth. "I'm getting older every minute. I think I've aged twenty years since yesterday! Just like the rest of you—''

"That's enough!" Aunt Flora called the meeting back to order. "Squabbling amongst ourselves won't get us anywhere. The point is: what are we to do about this situation?"

"What *can* we do?" Jennifer was serious, for once. "Father has presented us with a *fait accompli*. Game, set and match to Father. Especially match—" She began laughing again.

"Hysteria will get us nowhere," Aunt Flora reproved.

"I agree," Godfrey said. "The situation is too serious to be laughed off."

"What else can we do?" Jennifer pulled herself together with an effort. "Realistically, I mean. Reggie's pipe dreams about speeding cars are all very well, but things don't happen so conveniently in real life."

Unless someone makes them happen. The uncomfortable thought slid into my mind and would not be dismissed.

There was an uneasy silence in the room. Then Aunt Maddy cleared her throat and broke the spell.

"Quite right," she said. "We have been faced with an impossible situation; we now have to learn to live with it. Or, rather, her."

"She seems to be a pleasant sort," I defended tentatively. "It could have been a lot worse."

"Worse!" Tamar could have given Cromwell lessons in spitting at the moment. "How could it have been any worse?"

"Well," I pointed out thoughtfully, "I understand there are some States where a girl can get legally married at fourteen—"

Tamar turned her back on me. The others moved away. I was too young, too frivolous, too uncaring. If I were not careful, they would close ranks against me, as they were closing ranks against Wanda-Lu.

"I'm sorry," I said quickly. "I couldn't resist it."

They turned back, forgiving me, but still showing a certain reserve. My gesture towards partisanship had been noted and would not be forgotten. I was now caught between Scylla and Charybdis: Uncle Wilmer would insist that I be friends with his bride; the others would hold it against me if I succeeded.

"Of course " Aunt Flora lifted her head and stared into middle distance—"she'll never fit in. There are many little ways she could be made to realize it. I couldn't help noticing at dinner last night that she had obviously never seen a crown roast before."

"Perhaps Aunt Maddy ought to start serving artichokes more often." Jennifer's suggestion was only half-mocking.

"And samphire!" Tamar's eyes gleamed. "Even lots of English people don't know how to eat samphire."

The doorbell pealed and we all jumped guiltily.

"I'll go." I found I was relieved at the idea of getting out of that room, even for a few moments. The atmosphere had been getting oppressive. "It's probably one of the house guests coming back from a walk."

It was Davina. She stood at the door looking oddly subdued and unsure of her welcome.

"Come in." I found myself sympathetic. She had, after all, behaved like a thoroughbred last night. It would have been so easy for her to have pleaded a sudden headache and gone home. We would all have understood—

perhaps that was why she had not. Instead, she had sat grimly through the meal, forcing a smile.

"I hope I'm not intruding—" Despite her words, she walked past me, heading unerringly for the library. It made me wonder suddenly if she had been the one silently turning the doorknob recently. Had she stood outside the door listening? If so, how much had she heard?

"That's strange . . ." On her way through the drawing room, Davina halted by the coffee table where Uncle Wilmer's birthday gifts were still piled—he would open them at the big party tonight. "I'm sure someone's been moving those about—"

"It's all right." I took stock quickly counting. "They're all there." If any were missing, I wouldn't have been surprised. Feelings had been running high last night. It wouldn't have been astonishing if some of the family had snatched their presents back.

"No." She shook her head impatiently at my lack of comprehension. "I mean, they've been moved—"

"Oh . . ." I didn't see that it mattered. Someone might have picked up a parcel, considered removing it, then had second—and wiser—thoughts. Uncle Wilmer would keep a sharp mental tally of his supporters.

"Perhaps one of the dogs knocked them to the floor during the night." I spoke placating. "Then someone just piled them back on the table any old whichway this morning."

"Perhaps—" She had picked up her own present and was about to place it on top of the pile when she suddenly seemed to recall that it didn't matter any more. The jockeying for position was over; the prize had gone to a rank outsider. She let the box fall back on the table at the base of the pile and moved on.

The others greeted her as though she had a right to be there, admitting her into the conference . . . the conspiracy. As Godfrey had remarked earlier. "At least Davina would have been *suitable*."

Only Aunt Maddy seemed to be concealing some secret satisfaction. *The devil you know is better than the devil you don't know* was a highly suspect concept, I realized suddenly. Both Aunt Maddy and I knew what would have happened to us if Davina had become the new Lady Creighleigh. Whereas the unknown quantity was less of a danger.

Wanda-Lu was seventeen—and an alien. It was most unlikely that she would even consider changing the status quo. She would concentrate on fitting into the existing pattern of her elderly husband's life. It would not occur to her to make sweeping changes in order to emphasize her own position. Those of us most concerned would have nothing to fear from her. She was far less of a threat than Davina had been.

It was a new thought and I retreated to a far corner to contemplate it. No wonder Mrs. Keyes had been so fulsomely welcoming. (Davina would have given her short shrift too.) She had been the first to spot the weakness of the new lady of the house—and the strength of her own position if she could ingratiate herself quickly enough.

"Davina, dear—" Having nothing at stake herself, Aunt Flora welcomed her unrestrainedly. "How good of you to come around. We were just discussing . . . our little problem."

"I thought you might be," Davina said. "I saw them drive off about an hour ago."

So she was still keeping watch. The habit must be too ingrained to break by now. There were times when I suspected that she kept better tabs on Uncle Wilmer than on little Lynette. Which reminded me . . .

"Where's—?" I began, and just then she came into view outside the french windows. She appeared to be deep in conversation with Cromwell.

"She wanted to play with the cat," Davina said. "And I thought it would be better for her to stay outside—"

"It's a sorry business." Godfrey shook his head. "Sorry." He sounded as though he were apologizing to Davina.

"Yes—" Davina's gaze rested thoughtfully on her daughter. "He'll be sorry. But it isn't the end of the world." She brightened. "Sir Wilmer has simply made a frightful mistake. Everyone does at least once in a lifetime. After all—" she smiled forgivingly—"he's at an age when men do foolish things. They call it the male menopause, don't they?"

"At *his* age," Aunt Maddy snorted, "he's coming up to the male menopause for the second time around!"

"Second childhood, more likely!" Aunt Flora snapped. "Wilmer is living in a fool's paradise if he thinks this ridiculous marriage will last. I'll give it six months at best."

"Oh dear." Davina's hopeful face belied her mournful tone. She was reviving more every minute. "How sad . . . but I do fear you're right. The marriage can't last."

"The problem is," Aunt Maddy said, "that, at this pace, Wilmer may not last that long himself."

There was silence as we contemplated this.

"That *would* be unfortunate." Jennifer's eyes narrowed. "If anything happened to Father while he was still married to this girl, she'd stand to collect almost everything."

"Especially," Reggie pointed out cheerfully, "if he should die before making a new will. Right now, any previous will is invalidated by his marriage. You children wouldn't be left out in the cold entirely, of course, but you'd certainly be feeling the draught."

"Oh, you poor, poor dears!" Davina, in her self-appointed persona as almost stepmother, oozed sympathy, quite overlooking the fact that her own plans for the "poor dears" had almost certainly not included sharing any more of Uncle Wilmer's pelf than was absolutely necessary. "I *do* think it's so unfair of Sir Wilmer to inflict this on you. It's so—so undignified! A stepmother young enough to be your daughter."

Godfrey made a low growling noise in his throat. Jennifer's eyes were nearly slits. Aunt Maddy snorted with repressed amusement.

"Not quite," Tamar said. "Not in *my* case, anyway. I'd have had to be pretty quick off the mark to have a child that age."

"Oh, I wasn't referring to you, Tamar," Davina assured her. "I wouldn't presume to. Everyone knows you have such a marvelous *rapport* with the younger generation—"

She halted abruptly, suddenly aware that she had shown more of her claws than intended. She would not want to start her putative stepchildren thinking that they had perhaps had a lucky escape.

"We're all on edge and no wonder—" Aunt Flora intervened. "This is a frightful situation, but Reggie is right. Nothing must happen to that—that Wanda-Lu until Wilmer has made a new will with some sensible provisions."

"Nothing is likely to happen to Wanda-Lu," Aunt Maddy pointed out, "except boredom, chilblains and possibly frustration."

"Precisely!" Aunt Flora said triumphantly. "She'll never fit in here—and the sooner she discovers it, the better. It would really be a kindness to make her realize the fact."

"Just don't let Uncle Wilmer catch you at it!" I didn't expect the observation to make me popular, and it didn't. The others looked at me thoughtfully.

Rex got up and moved to the french windows, whimpering restively. Godfrey took it as his cue.

"Pippa," he said, as though just visited by an extremely bright thought, "why don't you take Rex out for a walk? In fact, why don't you take all the dogs?"

Because I'd rather stay here and listen to what you're plotting. But they knew that and had no intention of saying anything more in front of me. They didn't trust me not to go running to the enemy with it.

"Good idea!" Jennifer thrust Nell Gwynn at me, and Frou-Frou, who had been half asleep in Tamar's lap, sat up expectantly at the magic word "walk."

"Oh, all right." I was outvoted and I knew it, but I refused to hitch them up to leads and battle my way through the village. I opened the french windows. "Come on, you lot," I said ungraciously.

The dogs rushed into the garden, barking excitedly.

Cromwell spat viciously at them and darted for his favorite tree. Naturally the dogs chased such a tempting mobile target.

"They'll catch him! They'll catch him!" Lynette shrieked. "They'll tear him to bits!"

"Don't be silly," I said. "They won't hurt him, even if they do catch him. In any case, Cromwell can take care of himself."

Cromwell abruptly decided to prove my point. He halted in mid-flight, whirled about, and slashed out with his claws at the nearest nose. Frou-Frou fled, yelping; the other dogs withdrew to a more prudent distance. Fun was fun, but Cromwell wasn't taking the game in the proper spirit.

Cromwell sneered at them and climbed the tree in an insultingly leisurely manner. When he had attained his favorite perch in the topmost branches, he crouched there and spat down at the dogs again. Thus safely challenged, they rushed forward and circled the tree, barking loudly.

"Really, Pippa!" Tamar appeared in the french window behind me, nursing her injured pet. "Can't you keep any sort of order? All we asked was that you take the dogs out for a walk. It was a perfectly simple request. It didn't entail much effort on your part. But no, you couldn't do even that. You had to let them out into the garden to be attacked by that vicious cat. My poor Frou-Frou—"

It was *too* unfair. The dogs had started hostilities—and it was Cromwell's home, not theirs. I'd like to see Tamar try to control four excited animals at a moment's notice.

"Well, I'm sorry I'm so inefficient and useless," I said sarcastically. Hostility was in the air and I was not immune to it. I moved up to the window to fling my own challenge into the library.

"Better luck with the *next* member of the family! I'll bet it won't be too long before Wanda-Lu produces a new half-brother or half-sister for you. Perhaps you'll be able to train him—or her—to your standards of perfection. And the best of British luck to you!"

There was a short—dare I say pregnant?—silence, then Tamar gasped as though I had struck her across the face. Beyond her, the others registered shock and a dawning realization of the possibility I had just put forth.

I backed away from the window, suddenly guilt-stricken. Not because I had upset the others, but because I had abruptly realized that I might have put Wanda-Lu in even more jeopardy by my reckless remarks.

CHAPTER 10

I LEANED AGAINST THE TREE-TRUNK AND GLARED AT Cromwell. He glared down at me, but the glare was melting into complacency. The enemy was routed, his field was clear—except for me. And what did he have to fear from me?

Godfrey and Jennifer had whistled their dogs back to heel. Davina had swooped into the garden and borne Lynette away. I was the only one remaining—a pariah.

No one was going to invite me indoors. The subject under discussion was not for my possibly traitorous ears.

All in all, I was in a very bad mood.

"Shut up!" I snarled at Cromwell, as he hissed again. "You can just shut up! It's all your fault!"

The hissing continued and, when I glanced upwards angrily, I discovered that Cromwell had curled up, closed his eyes and was, to all intents and purposes, asleep.

I realized that the hissing had come from ground level, somewhere close to me. I looked around uncertainly.

"Sssstt!" There it was again. This time I was able to spot the source. Something pale and wand-like appeared, disappeared, and then reappeared from behind a bush. "SSsssstt!" It was a hand beckoning to me.

I approached the bush cautiously. The hand had disappeared again, but a sense of urgency still seemed to vibrate in the surrounding air.

"It took you long enough," Triffid complained as I reached him. "Your reflexes aren't very good, are they?"

"I happen to have a lot on my mind at the moment," I said coldly. I got enough criticism from the family, without complete strangers joining in. "What are you doing skulking about in the bushes, anyway?"

"I'm trying to keep a low profile," he said. "Whenever any of your family see me, they back me into a corner and try to pump me about Sir Wilmer's intentions. They must think I'm clairvoyant," he added bitterly. "I haven't had a chance to have one word with him yet—despite the fact that I was specifically requested to attend this weekend."

"Your father was requested," I pointed out. "It will

take Sir Wilmer a little while to adjust to the change in arrangements. He hates to have his plans disrupted.''

"He doesn't seem to mind what he does to anyone else's plans.'' The Triffid spoke with a certain grim satisfaction. I got the impression that he was not entirely displeased to be here, despite the occasional awkwardness. It must be a lot more exciting than the customary duties falling to a junior partner. He would be dining out on the story for a long time to come.

"Perhaps he thinks their plans shouldn't depend so much on him.'' It was true, although I hadn't given it much thought before. It would not be surprising, given Uncle Wilmer's notoriously short-tempered attitude towards fools, if he thought his own children should have grown up with more ability—and willingness—to stand on their own two feet. Since they showed no signs of this admirable attitude and still seemed more concerned about his money than their own, perhaps he secretly considered them fools.

"It's all right for you—'' The Triffid seemed to have picked up the prevailing attitude. "Your inheritance is quite safe. You needn't worry about the whims of a man who may have flipped over into senility when he was away from home and among strangers who wouldn't notice because they didn't have any experience of his behavioral norm.''

"If those are the ideas the family are pushing at you, I'd forget them,'' I warned. "There's nothing wrong with Uncle Wilmer. If you don't believe me, try that idea on your father before you try it on the Law Courts.''

"I never said anything about the Law Courts!'' The Triffid winced visibly and stepped backwards.

"No, and you'd better not, Triffid—er, um, Trifflin."

"Oh, I know what everyone calls me." It was obviously a long-standing grievance. "They called me that at school. But we're nearly of an age, you might call me Ian." He added, fatally, "Wanda-Lu does."

"Oh, really?" This time it was I who stepped back. "I had no idea you were on such close terms... and so quickly... *Ian*."

"You needn't take it like that," he said defensively. "Americans call everyone by their first names as soon as they meet. You must know that."

"I didn't," I said, "but no doubt I'll find out. At the moment, you're the only expert on Americans around here."

"I wouldn't say that." He had turned nasty. "I think that honor goes to your uncle. Hands down."

"Anyway—" It was time to call a truce. "What were you hissing at me about? I thought it was urgent, but it seems that all you want to do is quarrel."

"Oh, that," he said. "I just wanted to ask you a few questions. I thought we might have a reasonable conversation. I can see now that I was wrong. You're just like the rest of your family."

"Why shouldn't I be?" Those were fighting words. "And what's wrong with my family, anyway?"

"If you don't know—" he shook his head—"I haven't the time to go into it now. Perhaps, if you made an appointment—when you have a day or so to spare..."

I began to think that I had liked him better when he had seemed shy and intimidated. Unfortunately I didn't seem to produce that effect in him. "Perhaps I'll do that some day." I turned on my heel. "Why don't you just hold your breath while you're waiting?"

"Hold on!" he cried plaintively, as I started to walk away. "I wanted to ask you something."

"Ask then." I hesitated, making it plain that I was on my way elsewhere. "What is it?"

"I'm hungry," he whined. "Isn't there any place to eat around here? The pub in the village doesn't open for breakfast."

"There's the kitchen," I said. "You can help yourself."

"That's what your Cousin Tamar told me, but when I went out to the kitchen, I couldn't find any food."

"That's nonsense! The kitchen is full of food."

"Where?" he challenged me. "I found a cornflakes box, but it was full of soap-filled scouring pads. The egg box had some kind of seedling in each compartment and the milk carton was half-full of last night's gravy—" His voice was rising towards hysteria.

"That's Mrs. Keyes," I told him. "She housekeeps in her own inimitable way. Did you try the coal-scuttle? There were a couple of dozen fresh peaches in it."

"Yes," he said. "Of course I tried the coal-scuttle. Where else would anyone keep fresh peaches? But I couldn't even find the coal-scuttle this morning."

"She must have moved it again. Tamar shouldn't have sent you out to the kitchen on your own," I admitted. "But she has a lot on her mind right now." Which reminded me. "I don't suppose you've seen Toy Boy this morning, have you?"

"If you mean Danny—He gave me an odd look. "Danny Lora, yes, I saw him briefly. He wasn't interested in food. He was loading his camera just before setting out to follow the newlyweds. All he was worried about was getting some good pictures."

"He would be." That was what I had been afraid of.

"Fortescue, now, is the smart one." The Triffid continued brooding over his own paltry problem. "Do you know what he carries in that briefcase of his?" He didn't wait for my guesses. "A tin of pâté and a packet of crackers. A slab of chocolate and a half-flash of brandy. And a couple of paperbacks. He could hole up all weekend, if necessary. From now on, I'm taking a leaf from *his* book when I have to stay overnight or longer with clients. *I'm* going to turn *my* briefcase into a survival kit, too."

"How do you know?" I asked curiously. I had already guessed about the paperbacks, but I was impressed by his catalog of the rest of the contents. "Did he unpack it for you?"

"No, I was in the kitchen when he came sneaking in to throw away the pâté tin. The *empty* pâté tin," he added bitterly. "He threw it in the dustbin. Rather, he tried to. That was when we discovered where the potatoes were kept." Again bitterness overwhelmed him. "*Raw* potatoes."

"Oh, come on," I said impatiently. "I'll find you something to eat!"

"You're sure we're going in the right direction?" He followed me towards the kitchen. "Shouldn't we look in the potting-shed or some likely place like that?"

"It's just Mrs. Keyes's way of making herself indispensable," I explained. "If no one can ever find anything, she thinks we'll have to keep her on. She doesn't realize we can find everything if we look hard enough.

It's just a question of second-guessing her. I'm usually quite good at it.''

"You must be," he said gloomily, "or you'd have starved to death by now."

"It helps to think of it as a game," I said briskly. "If you weren't so hungry, you might find it stimulating. *We* often do." We often cursed Mrs. Keyes to high heaven, as well, but I wasn't telling him that.

"I was never amused by Hunt-the-Penny," he said stiffly. "Nor was I brought up to search strange houses."

"Weren't you lucky?"

Really, it was all quite straightforward. The rashers of raw bacon were neatly folded in the drawer of the coffee grinder; the eggs were in the spaghetti jar (a bit tricky rolling them out); the bread had remained in the biscuit tin; and the butter was actually in the fridge. Mrs. Keyes hadn't come up with any new tricks this time.

Down the hall, a door opened and muted voices could be heard. It seemed that the indignation meeting had broken up. I wondered just what mischief they had planned, then decided that it was better not to know.

"I don't want all that," the Triffid said. "We'll be having lunch soon now, won't we?"

"Why didn't you say so?" I tried to roll the eggs back into the spaghetti jar, but they slipped down too quickly, cracking themselves and the egg immediately beneath. How did Mrs. Keyes do it?

"Have you seen Jarvis?" Jennifer poked her head round the kitchen door. I noticed that she had combed her hair and freshened her lipstick. There was also a determined glint in her eyes. It occurred to me that she might have cut her losses where Uncle Wilmer was concerned and decided to sound out his bank manager as to the possibility of financing her dream with a mortgage. Another mortgage. She was already running a hefty one on her chic little Chelsea flat, despite the fact that Uncle Wilmer had given her a generous sum for the deposit.

"I haven't seen him." I turned towards the Triffid. "I believe you saw him last?"

"Briefly—" He met Jennifer's enquiring eyes. "About an hour ago. Er, he was on his way out. Er, for a walk."

"I see." Jennifer glanced at her watch. Automatically, I checked my own. The pub would be opening momentarily. It was always a fair bet that one could find strayed house guests there.

"Perhaps I'll take Nell for a run," Jennifer said thoughtfully. "The poor dear has been feeling a bit neglected lately, with all the other dogs around and that ruffian cat."

"They started it—" I sprang too Cromwell's defense, but Jennifer wasn't waiting to argue. She nodded vaguely and withdrew, presumably to collect her dog and continue her pursuit of Jarvis Fortescue.

"Er, the toast seems to be burning—" the Triffid interrupted my train of thought. "I thought it was supposed to pop up automatically."

"It is." I moved to discover what was wrong. "It must have stuck—oh!" The smell drifting upwards in a cloud of smoke bore only a partial resemblance to that of burning bread. As I reached the toaster, flames began coming out of the top.

"Don't touch it!" Moving with unexpected speed and resourcefulness, the Triffid jerked the plug from the electrical connection in the wall and looked around. The towel rack was empty. On form, the tea-towels were probably rolled up and hidden in the coffee canister.

Before I could move, the Triffid snatched up a cardigan draped over the back of a chair and dropped it over the flaming toaster.

"That's Mrs. Keyes's cardigan!" I gasped. "You shouldn't have used that. She'll have a fit!"

"Serves her right," he said grimly. "The flames had to be smothered. And it's all her fault, isn't it?"

"Probably." He was catching on fast. "But we can't be sure until we check. There might have been a fault in the wiring—"

"There might." He didn't believe it for a minute and, really, neither did I.

A large scorch mark had appeared across the back of the cardigan and smoke was curling out beneath the edges, but the smoke appeared to be lessening. After a moment, it had almost died away. The danger appeared to be over.

"Now let's see what happened." He lifted the cardigan carefully and, lest it be smoldering, tossed it into the sink.

A final cloud of smoke had billowed upwards with the removal of the cardigan. It dissipated into the air, leaving a strange odor behind.

"Thank you," I said, as we waited for the toaster to cool to the point where we could investigate it. "That was fast work. It could have got very nasty."

"Right." He didn't so much as brush my thanks aside as ignore it completely. "Now let's see what the trouble was."

I found a skewer hanging on the pan rack and we

delicately probed the toaster. The charred slices of bread slid out more or less easily, but there was a disgusting glutinous residue at the bottom.

"Whatever that mess is, I don't think we're going to shift it without a battle," Ian Trifflin said. "What's it doing in there, anyway?"

"Could it be rubber bands?" I asked doubtfully. It didn't smell particularly like rubber. "I suppose Mrs. Keyes hid it there." I answered his question belatedly. "She's never done that with the toaster before. Of course, she's been more insecure than usual this week."

"She ought to be sacked," he said harshly. "This was bloody dangerous." As he spoke, he managed to dislodge a piece of the sticky mess. It left long strings of itself along the wire coils before it fell out on the counter. We looked at it blankly.

"I think—" after a long moment, I hazarded a guess at its identity—"I think it's a wine gum. Little Lynette lost a packet of them the other day. Mrs. Keyes must have found them and popped them into the toaster before she left last night. It was all right when we used it yesterday morning."

"It's hard to imagine that a grown woman could be so irresponsible," he said. "Are you sure the child didn't put them in there herself?"

"Lynnie wouldn't do a thing like that," I said. "She's really quite a bright child. She'd know better."

"Of course she would!" I had not heard Davina come in. She stood beside me now, staring down at the sticky blob. "Lynette would never dream of doing such thing. It's that Keyes woman. She's half-mad. And now the toaster is ruined!"

"It's my fault." I hurried to be placatory. Perhaps I was the only one to hear the footsteps coming down the hall. "I should have turned the toaster upside down and shaken it before I put the bread in."

"Don't be absurd, Pippa, you shouldn't have done anything of the sort!" Davina snapped. "This house should be run on a normal footing. That woman will have to go!"

"Good morning, madam." Mrs. Keyes spoke in forbidding tones from the doorway.

"I mean it." Davina paled, but she stood her ground. "She'll have to go!"

"Ah, well." Mrs. Keyes stalked into the kitchen. "That's not for *you* to say, is it, *madam*?"

CHAPTER 11

"IT'S A NICE LITTLE PUB," THE TRIFFID ADMITTED, settling down our drinks and sinking into the chair beside me. "If we stay here until closing time, do you think it will be safe to go back to the house then?"

"It's perfectly safe now," I said. "It isn't us Mrs. Keyes is mad at—it's Davina."

"Hmmm." He didn't sound too confident. He was a

"Mrs. Keyes won't make any scenes today." I was

trying to convince myself as much as him. "She's on her best behavior, trying to impress Wanda-Lu. She doesn't have to worry about Davina any more. It's Wanda-Lu who's the mistress of the house."

"Not very pleased about it, are they?" He gave me a sharp look. "Any of your relatives, I mean."

"Can you blame them? It's especially upsetting for my cousins to be presented with a stepmother who's almost half their own age."

"Happens all the time in some circles. If Sir Wilmer had made his pile a lot earlier, he might be on his third or fourth young wife by now. Your cousins would have become hardened to it."

"Try telling that to my cousins," I said coldly. "I'm sure they'd be comforted to hear it."

"Oh, I know it's a shock—" He allowed his gaze to stray towards the far corner where Jennifer was tête-à-tête with Jarvis Fortescue. She was rolling her eyes at him in a way that seemed excessive in one working for a second mortgage. He was absently feeding crisps to Nell Gwynn under the table.

"To say the least—"

"But it might do them a world of good. It's high time they stopped counting on the old boy's money and got on with their own lives."

"Coming from someone who's just stepped into a partnership in *his* father's business, that's rich!"

"It's not the same thing at all," he said heatedly. "I've studied for it, passed my exams, and I'm actively contributing to the business. I'm not a parasite sitting around waiting for someone to die."

"So that's your opinion of my family!" I drew myself

up, but the promising battle was cut short before I could loose my next volley. The Saloon Bar door swung open and Uncle Wilmer and Wanda-Lu walked in, silencing every conversation in the pub.

"Speak of the devil," Ian Trifflin said softly. "It doesn't look as though he's anxious to get back to the house, either."

"Congratulations, Sir Wilmer!" someone called out. Others took up the cry. The landlord came forward, beaming a welcome.

"Thank you, thank you." Uncle Wilmer advanced in triumphal progress, Wanda-Lu clinging to his arm, her eyes shining. It all went to his head. "I'll ask you all to join me in drinking to my good fortune," he announced.

There was a rush to the bar, during which Uncle Wilmer took over the best table. He nodded regally to me and then to Jennifer, but did not motion us to join him.

Not that there would have been room for us. After collecting their drinks at the bar, the well-wishers gathered around the bridal pair, raising their glasses in toasts. Soon they were so surrounded they were lost to sight. Wanda-Lu's little shrieks of delight could be heard above the raucous laughter.

Jennifer frowned and leaned forward to murmur something to Jarvis Fortescue. He nodded agreement and they rose and left. I wasn't the only one to notice. Sly, sidelong glances followed them to the door. The regulars were going to have a great old gossip once we were all out of the way.

I had been tempted to leave myself but now, of course, I couldn't. There were too many eyes watching, too many people ready to jump to the wrong conclusion if I did. I would have to stay put until the crowd around Uncle Wilmer and Wanda Lu thinned and then go over and join them for a final drink.

A movement outside the window caught my eye, then the whole window darkened as someone pressed against it. Someone was trying to see into the taproom, but the small square panes were the pseudo-bottle-glass distorting type and impossible to see through. They let in a bit of outside light, but that was about all. Idly I watched the shadowy head bob about, trying for a clear view, and made a mental bet with myself.

I won. After a moment Toy Boy appeared in the doorway and moved into the room, blinking in the sudden gloom.

"Danny—" Ian raised his hand—"over here!"

Toy Boy came straight to our table and sat down with obvious relief. I realized that he had disliked the prospect of walking into a room full of people who were not only strangers, but also friends of Uncle Wilmer's. He had probably been visualizing the loss of another camera.

As it was, he lowered the camera into his lap and began unscrewing the telephoto lens. He would not need it at this range.

"Had a busy and successful morning?" Ian enquired.

"Busy, anyway." Toy Boy slid a light meter out of its case and laid it inconspicuously on the table. "And you?" He asked automatically and without interest, preoccupied with sorting out the proper filter from another case.

"Fascinating. Can I get you a drink?"

"Pint of ale, thanks."

"Do you really expect to be able to get any pictures in here?" I asked, as the Triffid left to get the drink.

"It's not all that dark." He squinted at the reading on the light meter. "This filter ought to do it."

"I don't mean the darkness," I told him. "I mean Uncle Wilmer. When the crowd clears enough for you to focus, he'll be able to see you. It's not like crouching behind bushes and catching him unawares."

"Don't worry, he's not unaware," Toy Boy said bitterly. "He's been aware all morning. And he's ruined every shot. The old bastard is a genius at moving just when I trip the shutter. All I've got is a collection of blurs."

"Good for Uncle Wilmer! After all, you can't blame him for wanting some privacy on his honeymoon. He didn't expect to come back and find a press photographer living in his own home."

"I'm living over the garage—if you can call it living. It's not quite what I expected when Tamar invited me down for the weekend."

"Didn't she warn you that her family were old-fashioned?"

"Yes, but I didn't know she meant antediluvian. Oh, thanks." Ian had set his pint down before him. "Anyway, I've fallen into a great story. You can't expect me not to make the most of it."

"You can try," I said. "But I think you'd do better to wait until Wilmer is willing to co-operate. When he's ready, he'll call a Press Conference and you can all—"

"With the rest of Fleet Street and the International mob? No, thanks. I've got an exclusive right now and that's the way I'm keeping it. Even if he smashes up another camera."

"Which he very well might." The crowd was thinning around Uncle Wilmer's table now. Any minute he was going to look across and find Toy Boy aiming that lens at him. Worse, he was going to find me consorting with the enemy. Perhaps, if I got up now and started over towards his table, he might think Toy Boy had arrived after I left...

A general intake of breath stopped me just as I was rising from my seat. I followed the combined gaze of the regulars and sat down again abruptly. Suddenly it seemed more prudent to stay where I was.

Davina advanced upon the bar slowly but unfalteringly. She seemed faintly puzzled by the moderate sensation her presence had created. Uncle Wilmer's table was still concealed, so she could not know the reason for it.

"Orange juice and crisps," she ordered clearly. "And a large brandy."

The customers surrounding Uncle Wilmer melted away and, for the first time, she had an unobstructed view of the whole room. The silence deepened and the landlord hastened to produce the orange juice and crisps.

"There you are," he said, too loudly and too jovially. "Your little girl is outside, is she?"

"Yes." Davina had paled, but she rallied and picked up the ordered refreshments. "I'll just give these to her—"

The hum of conversation resumed as she crossed to the doorway and handed out the orange juice and crisps. She walked stiffly, her back straight. She looked as though she would like to cut and run. She would have everyone's sympathy if she did.

"I won't be long, darling," her voice carried back into the room. "You stay right there."

Lynette's reply was indistinguishable, then Davina turned and went back to the bar. The landlord had her double brandy waiting.

"No, no," he said, as she fumbled for her change purse. "It's on Sir Wilmer. We're drinking his health and good fortune. Isn't that right, Sir Wilmer?"

"Yes, yes, indeed." Uncle Wilmer was, quite rightly, embarrassed. Everyone in the room was accustomed to seeing him as Davina's escort. They knew as well as he did what had been expected of him. Again, sly sidelong glances marked his every move.

"Thank you, Sir Wilmer." Davina's voice barely trembled. She had had a chance to get some practice in last night. She had known this public moment must come, but had not expected it quite so soon. She raised her glass. "Your very good health."

"You mean you've left your sweet li'l girl outside?" Wanda-Lu was incredulous. "Why don't you bring her in to join the party?"

"It's against the law," Uncle Wilmer said quickly, obviously relieved that a neutral subject had been broached. "Licensing laws. Children not allowed in pubs. Have to wait outside. Can't step over the threshold until they're fourteen—and then they aren't allowed to order anything alcoholic."

"Well, I don't think that's fair." Wanda-Lu might have been even more upset if Uncle Wilmer had not withheld the information that, strictly speaking, she was not eligible to be served alcohol herself until after her eighteenth birthday. "This is such a nice peaceful place, there's no reason at all why a child shouldn't be in here. It's a lot more orderly than some restaurants I've known— and they let kids in them.''

"I quite agree." Davina had had time to recover. "However, the law is the law. It may be changed some day to accord with the rest of the Common Market, but right now I'm afraid that Lynette has to wait outside while I have my drink."

"And that poor child is out there all alone!" Wanda-Lu stood up decisively. "I'll just go out and say hello to her." She paused at the bar. "Yes, and I'll have a nice big bag of potato chips, too, none of those little bitty bags." The landlord almost threw it at her in his haste. She took it and went outside.

"Wanda-Lu is very fond of children," Uncle Wilmer said into the silence that followed.

Davina bared her teeth at him in a travesty of a smile. Then, as though conscious that something more might be required in order to paper over the social cracks, she picked up her glass and went over to sit at his table.

There was another faint *click*. I became aware that I had been conscious of a muted clicking sound for quite some time. I turned accusingly to Toy Boy.

"I hope you've got enough pictures for your story."

"I think so." He did not recognize any irony. "And about time, too. The old boy's led me a merry chase all morning. He owes me a few."

"I doubt if he realizes he's been paying his debt."

"Shouldn't think so." Toy Boy gave a laugh that was almost a snicker. "He's got more on his mind right now."

He certainly had and he was beginning to look as

though it was weighing heavily on him. Davina, her face still frozen in that grisly parody of a social smile, had begun talking softly to him as soon as the well-wishers had moved out of earshot. She barely moved her lips and no sound carried beyond them, but it was obvious that she had quite a bit to say.

Uncle Wilmer, also trying to keep a pleasant expression on his face, was losing the battle and growing more thunderous-looking. I realized that this was the first chance Davina had had to speak to him alone since his return. Neither of them, appeared to be enjoying the experience.

"I wouldn't like to be in his shoes." Toy Boy gave a gratified chortle, relishing Uncle Wilmer's discomfort. "She's really laying down the law to him."

"It's a mistake," I said thoughtfully. Davina had never shown Uncle Wilmer the shrewish side of her nature before; it was a serious error to reveal it now. Especially if the family were cooking up plans to make life so uncomfortable for Wanda-Lu that she would leave. They might manage to drive her away, but that was no guarantee that Uncle Wilmer would then fall into Davina's waiting arms. Not after the taste of Davina's temper he was getting now.

"Well, that's her problem, isn't it?" Toy Boy restored his camera to its case cheerfully. "I've got enough in here. I'll try for some nice domestic shots around the house this afternoon."

"That ought to make for a lively afternoon." Uncle Wilmer was already sliding into the worst possible mood. I knew the signs only too well. The fact that he had brought it on himself would never be acknowledged.

Instead, he would look around for someone he could blame. An incautious photographer—already in disfavor—would be a heavensent scapegoat.

"Wouldn't it be wiser to—?" I broke off. Wanda-Lu had come back into the pub and was standing beside me.

"Do you mind if I sit here with you for a minute?" she asked. "It looks kinda private over there right now."

"Of course." The Triffid leaped to his feet. "Let me get you a drink. Toy Boy had to remain seated, pinned down by his scattered bits of equipment, but he pulled out a chair for her.

"Yes, please do. It's so nice to see you again. Did you have a pleasant morning?" I was babbling in an attempt to hold her attention and divert her from the scene at Uncle Wilmer's table.

"Just fine—up to now." She wasn't fooled. She sank into the chair, her gaze rested thoughtfully on her husband, then moved to Davina. "She's very pretty, in an over-sophisticated way, isn't she? And she's got a darling little kid—"

"It was gin and tonic, right?" Ian set the drink in front of her. As he did so, Uncle Wilmer seemed to notice for the first time that she had returned.

"Why thank you, Ian. You're jes' so thoughtful—and observant, too." She fluttered her eyelashes at him, blatantly flirting, then turned to Toy Boy.

"I do hope you got some nice pictures this morning, Danny. I'm afraid Wilmer wasn't on his best behavior. I saw him spoiling your shots. It wasn't fair. We'll have to make it up to you some way. I know," Wanda-Lu clapped her hands, a girlish gesture I had read about but never seen executed in real life. It had the effect of focusing all attention on her.

"You can be our official wedding photographer!" She laid her hand lightly on Toy Boy's arm and beamed at him. "We never did get any proper pictures taken. You can take them now. How about that? Will you do it?"

In the distance, Uncle Wilmer twitched visibly. He couldn't hear what she was saying, but the gestures were clear. His bride was sitting with two men close to her own age and obviously enjoying herself. Uncle Wilmer stood up abruptly. Davina lost whatever last remnant of his attention she had had.

Of course, practically any man was going to be closer to Wanda-Lu's age than Uncle Wilmer was. It was a fact of life he was going to have to learn to live with. And one which Wanda-Lu would not be above exploiting occasionally.

I was overcome with admiration for her technique. She had brought Uncle Wilmer back to her side as nearly as if she had lassooed him and dragged him across the room. Furthermore, he was certain that it was his own idea. It was clear that the family might be taking on a more formidable opponent than they imagined.

"Wilmer, honey—" She greeted him with a sunny smile. "I was jes' telling Danny here that he's *got* to take some proper wedding photographs of us. I want to send some to my family—and I'm sure *your* family will want some, too."

I glanced sharply at her and was relieved to see that she didn't believe it for a minute. She was well aware that the last thing in the world any of her stepchildren wanted was her picture. Their ambition was to sweep her under the carpet, not display her photo on the mantel.

I now knew that it wasn't going to be as easy as they thought.

"We'll see." Uncle Wilmer used the time-honored phrase for quieting a demanding child. He was glowering at Toy Boy and Wanda-Lu was wise enough not to continue pushing him.

"Are you—" he spoke with the exquisite courtesy that stopped just short of sarcasm—"are you ready to leave yet?"

"More than ready." Wanda-Lu smiled and rose. "I'm anxious to leave. I'd like to get home and lie down and rest for a while. I seem to have a little bitty headache starting."

At least Toy Boy waited until they were out of earshot before saying, "I'll bet he's going to hear a lot of that line in the future."

"Well—" Davina was passing our table and had caught the remark. She could not resist replying. "He's brought it on himself."

CHAPTER 12

THE HOUSE WAS CURIOUSLY DESERTED WHEN WE returned. I paused in the hallway, listening. There was not a whisper of a human voice, not the faintest whimper from one of the dogs.

I stepped into the drawing room. It was empty. The library door at the far end was open and I could see that the library was unoccupied, too.

I knew that Uncle Wilmer and Wanda-Lu had returned earlier. They must be upstairs. But where had everyone else gone?

"I'll just pop over to my room and reload," Toy Boy said. "Perhaps Wanda-Lu will coax the old boy into a better mood—" he glanced upwards meaningly—"and I can strike while the iron is hot."

He left without waiting for an answer—or without looking around for Tamar, I noticed. She was not going to be pleased to find herself replaced by her father as the center of his attention. Even if she did invite Toy Boy down here with the idea of letting him get some exclusive pictures. The reality was too far a cry from the sedate birthday celebrations she had envisaged him capturing on film.

A faint plaintive wail drifted in on the breeze from the garden. Cromwell, still bemoaning his fate. There must be someone nearby to hear or he wouldn't be wasting his time complaining.

The Triffid followed me into the garden. He seemed to have decided that I was less awe-inspiring than the rest of the family—or perhaps that I'd protect him from them if he stuck close to me.

It certainly seemed as though someone out in the garden needed protection but, at first glance, it was not immediately apparent which one.

Godfrey and Uncle Wilmer were deep in conversation—

perhaps conflict—under Cromwell's tree. Godfrey had his fists clenched; Uncle Wilmer was wearing his most dangerously icy smile. Above them, Cromwell wailed softly of neglect and insupportable invasion of territory. Rex sat beside the tree-trunk and regarded Cromwell's histrionics with a disdainful air.

"Ah, Pippa and Young Ian!" Uncle Wilmer greeted us as reinforcements. "Just what we need—" he turned back to Godfrey—"a legal mind we can bend to our little problem."

Young Ian began to look wary. He was getting the measure of Uncle Wilmer and quite rightly suspected that *bend* was going to be the operative word.

"Come and see Godfrey's mind at rest." He gestured Ian to his side, I followed more slowly. "Assure Godfrey that I have my facts correct. He's worried about my financial arrangements. In fact, he has been kind enough to be concerned about them for quite some time now." Uncle Wilmer's voice sharpened. "Especially the posthumous ones."

"I don't think we should discuss this with—" Godfrey began.

"With my legal adviser?" Uncle Wilmer's eyes widened in simulated surprise. "Why ever not? I should say that he was eminently qualified to join in any such discussion."

Godfrey made a gesture of despair, somewhat marred by the fact that his hand was still clenched into a fist. From a distance, the gesture could have looked threatening.

"Come now," Uncle Wilmer continued. "I don't understand what you want. You can't have it all ways. I've tried to do my very best for you—"

"Your best?" Godfrey choked.

"My *very* best," Uncle Wilmer corrected, wounded. "I have just been explaining the Facts of Life to Godfrey." He included us in the conversation. "Financial life, I mean. I dealt with the rest of it quite some time ago. Capital Transfer Tax, as it now stands, to be exact. Godfrey appears to find it as distasteful as he found our earlier discussion when he was an adolescent."

"Your—" Godfrey bit off the next word.

"I am a reasonable and logical man," Uncle Wilmer said. "Like you, I am opposed to the idea of the Government annexing a large portion of my estate upon my inevitable demise. Therefore, I have taken the reasonable and logical step to prevent it."

Godfrey ground his teeth. It was obvious that there was rather a lot he'd like to say—if only he dared.

"Correct me if I'm wrong, Ian—" Uncle Wilmer's tone admitted of no such possibility. "I believe that, upon the death of one partner in a marriage, the entire estate passes to the surviving spouse without payment of Capital Transfer Tax."

"That's true," Ian admitted carefully. "The tax becomes payable upon the death of the survivor."

"Quite so." Uncle Wilmer beamed upon him. "And if that surviving spouse should then remarry, both partners could enjoy the full benefit of the estate. The tax position would not be affected."

"The bill certainly wouldn't be presented upon remarriage." Ian was still proceeding cautiously. "It's not like alimony arrangements which cease when the ex-partner remarries. The tax bill wouldn't be due until—" He broke off abruptly.

"There you have it!" Uncle Wilmer was so pleased

with himself, he did not notice the expression on Ian's face. "That's what I've been explaining to Godfrey. It's perfectly simple. I have married a young and healthy woman who is unlikely to predecease me. When, in the fullness of time—much time, I hope—I am gathered to my reward, she will still be quite young and attractive. She will also be a rich widow. It is unthinkable that she should fall prey to some fortune-hunter and the estate pass out of the family. What more natural, then, than that Godfrey should marry her himself?"

"It's not natural!" Godfrey said, agonized. "It's appalling! It's immoral! And furthermore," he added, spotting a ray of hope, "it's against the law!"

"Nonsense!" Uncle Wilmer said. "Morality is simply a question of geography. Things that are illegal in one corner of the world are permissible—sometimes laudable— in another corner. It will simply be a matter of judicious enquiry and then the purchase of a pair of airline tickets to the right destination. Even you should be able to cope with it."

"No!" Godfrey said.

"You'll have plenty of time to think it over," Uncle Wilmer pointed out. "You'll get used to the idea. Your sisters will help you adjust to it. I'm sure they'll approve."

They would, too. Just as soon as they realized it was a way of keeping all the money without paying any tax, Godfrey would be hearing the strains of the "Wedding March" before the the "Funeral March" had died away.

"What does Wanda-Lu think of the idea?" I asked.

"Oh . . ." For the first time, Uncle Wilmer looked uneasy. "Actually, I haven't mentioned the idea to her.

Umm, perhaps it would be as well if no one raised the subject until . . . until I'm gone.''

I could see his point. It wasn't exactly the sort of sweet nothing a bride would care to have whispered into her ear during the honeymoon. Or at any other time, for that matter. Uncle Wilmer might well boggle at the thought of introducing the subject. How could he go about it? ("By the way, darling, I'm bequeathing you to my son . . .")

"Oh, well, that will be a long time in the future, I'm sure," I said tactfully.

"*Are* you so sure, Pippa?" Uncle Wilmer gave me a bright, faintly malicious look. "That's nice to hear. When did you decide that? When you found you hadn't needed all that travel insurance on me, after all?"

So that was it! I looked back at him speechlessly as it all became clear to me. The whole ridiculous justification of his marriage he had just been inflicting on poor Godfrey was an absurd farrago. He hadn't been thinking about Capital Transfer Tax when he married Wanda-Lu; he had been salving his own bruised ego.

All of us—his sister, his children, his next-door neighbor—had spent the weeks before his departure impressing his age upon him. I, too, had been guilty. I hadn't actually *said* anything but, as he had just reminded me, actions speak louder than words. I had insured him up to the hilt—and he had noticed and resented it.

We were all guilty. We had all done our best—or worst—to make him feel that he had one foot in the grave and the other on a banana peel. It was small wonder he had looked around for a way to cock a snook at us. And he had found Wanda-Lu.

"I won't do it!" Godfrey said again, still following his own train of thought.

Of course he wouldn't. If the random thought ever crossed his mind, Uncle Wilmer had now made certain that it would be unthinkable. Perhaps that was what he had intended all along.

"Mmmrrryah!" Tiring of his self-imposed martyr's role, Cromwell leapt from his branch to Uncle Wilmer's shoulder. He swayed perilously for a moment, tightened his claws in Uncle Wilmer's jacket for purchase and then settled down, rubbing his head against Uncle Wilmer's ear.

"There, there, my beautiful boy—" Uncle Will's hand came up to stroke Cromwell. "You love me for myself alone, don't you, my beauty?"

He turned and strolled off towards the house and the open french window of the library, the cat riding on his shoulder. We looked after him silently.

"He's out of his mind!" Godfrey was still protesting. "It's the most obscene idea I've ever heard. I won't do it!"

"Oh, do be quiet!" I said in exasperation. "You don't have to do it. He's only been getting at you. At all of us."

"Do you really think so?" Godfrey began to calm down. "Well—" indignation took over from moral outrage—"I don't think it was funny. Not one bit."

"I'm not sure," I said slowly, "that he was intending to be funny."

"There are moments when I think—" Godfrey broke off, raised his head glumly to watch his father's progress across the lawn and into the library—"when I think the only possible solution would be if they were out driving and the car went over a cliff!''

''That would actually be most unsatisfactory, er, from your financial point of view,'' Ian said. ''In such accident cases, the well-established legal precedent is to consider that the younger—and presumably stronger—person will survive, however momentarily, the older and weaker. Therefore, it would be assumed that your father had predeceased his bride and the estate would devolve upon her, to be passed on, through her, to her own legal heirs. Thus, the estate would be liable for two lots of Capital Transfer tax and—''

''All right, all right!'' Godfrey cut off the lecture. ''I get the picture. You mean all *our* money—what was left of it—would go to *her* family in America, if that happened.''

''Oh, er, I shouldn't like to be that dogmatic about it. There are a number of variables. But I would suggest that it is preferable that the lady remain alive.''

''Thank you,'' Godfrey snarled. ''I've *got* the picture. Besides,'' he added regretfully, ''there aren't any cliffs around here, anyway.''

''Just make sure,'' I said, ''that the rest of the family gets the picture, too.''

''What do you mean? No!'' Godfrey raised his hand, cutting me off. ''Never mind.'' He snapped his fingers, bringing Rex to heel. ''We can discuss it later.'' His tone told me that we'd never mention it again. ''I must go now. I—I have a severe headache.''

''I'm afraid I've upset him,'' Ian said as Godfrey stalked away. ''But I was only trying to clarify the position for him so that he—''

"If you'll excuse me—" I didn't really care whether he did or not. "I have a headache coming on myself. I must go and see if I can find something for it."

The house was stirring now. I could hear the shrill yap of Frou-Frou somewhere upstairs, so Tamar was home. The heavy tread of Godfrey's progress along the upper hallway was setting the chandelier to shaking. Aunt Maddy's voice sounded from the front doorstep.

The green baize door to the kitchen hallway was still swinging slightly. It was a fairly safe bet that Uncle Wilmer had taken Cromwell through to the kitchen and was comforting him with tasty tit-bits.

I steadfastly ignored Ian Trifflin, who was still drifting along in my wake, and began mounting the stairs. I was aware that he was hovering at the foot of the stairs, watching me. Then I heard just the ghost of a resigned sigh as he gave up and went back into the drawing room.

Jennifer was coming along the hallway as I reached the top of the stairs. She was humming under her breath and did not appear to notice me until she had almost collided with me. She halted abruptly and gave me an accusing look.

"Why didn't you tell me Jarvis Fortescue was a widower?" she asked.

"I didn't know," I said truthfully.

"Well, he is. His wife died two years ago. I'd had no idea—"

"Neither had I." But she was no longer listening to me. Almost visibly, her mind wandered elsewhere. Her eyes unfocused and turned inwards. She gave a small nod of agreement to herself and continued along the hallway, leaving a trail of freshly-applied scent. She began humming again.

With a mental shrug, I continued on my own way. By now, my headache was beginning to make itself felt. It probably served me right. I tried to ignore the intensifying throb at my temples. It was becoming more difficult with every step.

I detoured into the bedroom at the end of the hall and rummaged through the medicine cabinet for the bottle of aspirins. I could not find it. I was sure I had seen it here the other day.

I pushed aside Tamar's lotions, Jennifer's shampoo, Godfrey's toothpaste and a collection of assorted vitamin pills and patent medicines. But I found nothing so simple as aspirins.

Then I remembered that Wanda-Lu had been talking about a headache. Perhaps she had walked away with the aspirins, although it was hard to see why she should have done so. Uncle Wilmer was the only one in the family with his own bathroom *en suite*. His medicine cabinet was always well-stocked. Perhaps he'd taken his own aspirins to the States with him and so Wanda-Lu had had to go on the scrounge for some wherever she could find them.

In that case, I would go and scrounge them back from her. It might be a shame to disturb her when she was resting but, by this time, I'd match my headache against anyone's and I needed those aspirins.

I tapped perfunctorily on the door of Uncle Wilmer's bedroom and entered without waiting for an invitation. Wanda-Lu was lying on top of the spread—still wearing her shoes, I noticed. Mrs. Keyes would have had a word or two to say about that, if she had seen it.

"Just passing through," I called out softly. "We seem to be out of aspirins in the family bathroom, so I thought I'd borrow some of yours." Without waiting for an answer, I continued through to the bathroom and opened the medicine cabinet.

"Oh—" In the tilt of the mirror, I saw Wanda-Lu struggle to a sitting position and swing her feet to the floor.

"Don't get up," I said. "It's all right. I know where everything is. I won't be a minute."

"Oh, but—" She appeared in the doorway behind me just as I found the bottle of aspirins and opened it. "I don't think you ought to use any of *them*. They look funny. Unless aspirins are awfully different in this country, I think they've gone bad or something."

"Gone bad?" I echoed incredulously. "I've never heard of such a thing. And anyway, how can you tell?" Presumably aspirins, like any other medicine, could lose their potency after a long period but, so far as I knew, there were no visible signs of this.

"Well, I didn't take any," she said stubbornly. "And I don't think you should. Just look at them."

I was already tipping some of the aspirins into my hand. I stared down at them, still incredulous.

"There!" Wanda-Lu said triumphantly. "You mean to tell me English aspirins *ought* to look like that?"

"No," I said. "They certainly oughtn't to." Instead of the familiar white tablets, these were pale brown and smaller. Even if the aspirins had shrunk with age, surely they would not have undergone such a strange color change. And yet, there was something familiar about them.

"I didn't think so." Wanda-Lu shook her head dubiously. "I know things can be different over here, but I didn't think they could be *that* different. So I put them back and decided I'd just lie down and try to take a nap instead."

"Just as well." I stared down at the strange nostrums, trying to identify them. Whatever they were, they certainly didn't belong in an aspirin container. Had Mrs. Keyes been extending her sphere of would-be influence? She had never breached Uncle Wilmer's quarters before. But what could these possibly—? And then I recognized them.

Slug pellets. I gasped in consternation.

"What is it?" Wanda-Lu asked anxiously.

"Nothing." I tried to keep my hand steady as I poured the slug pellets back into the aspirin container and capped it firmly. What Wanda-Lu didn't know wouldn't hurt her. Or should she be put on her guard?

"I'll just throw these out," I said. "We'll get fresh aspirins next time we go to the shops." I hoped my voice sounded unconcerned. Even if Wanda-Lu had taken the things in mistake for aspirin, they probably wouldn't have killed her. On the other hand, it was unlikely that they would have done her any good.

"I'll just have a word with Aunt Maddy."

CHAPTER 13

"I NEVER! I NEVER!" MRS. KEYES DREW HERSELF UP indignantly. "What would I want to do a thing like that for?"

What did she do anything for? Aunt Maddy and I exchanged hopeless glances. Even if she *had* done it, she would never admit it.

But we had to make a protest. This matter was too serious to overlook. Perhaps we had already let her get away with too much, just for the sake of keeping the peace.

"I never, never touch nothing in Sir Wilmer's rooms—" A long-standing grievance tinged her voice. "He'd never let me. You know that. He'd have my guts for garters!"

He would, too. There had been one memorable explosion the first—and only—time Mrs. Keyes had ventured into his quarters and disturbed all the piles of papers on his desk. She had been afraid he was going to do her actual physical injury—and so had we.

I suspected that, in their different ways, each of them had enjoyed the stormy scene. However, the lesson had been learned and Mrs. Keyes had confined her disruptive activity to the kitchen after that. It was unlikely that she would have done anything to jeopardize her position now. On the contrary, she had appeared to be making a positive effort to curry favor with the new lady of the house.

But who else would have done such a thing?

"That child plays over here more than she does in her own house," Mrs. Keyes said. "Perhaps she's been fooling around. *He* let *her* go everywhere!"

"Lynette does *not* play in Sir Wilmer's rooms," Aunt Maddy said crisply. "You know perfectly well they're out of bounds to all of us."

"I know they're *supposed* to be," Mrs. Keyes said darkly. "But he's spoiled that child rotten. She'd go in if she wanted to and never give it a second thought."

"But she wouldn't stay in there." I was certain of that. "Not long enough to muck things about. And she couldn't even reach the medicine cabinet."

"She could if she climbed up on the basin—" Mrs. Keyes was not going to give up easily, although not even she believed what she was saying.

"Lynette would never do that!" Aunt Maddy wasn't giving up either. There was a trace of desperation in her voice. I could understand why.

Those slug pellets hadn't got into the aspirin container by themselves. If Mrs. Keyes hadn't put them there, then who had?

Was this the opening shot in the campaign to be waged by the family to drive Wanda-Lu away?

Yet Aunt Maddy honestly seemed to know nothing about it—and she had been present at the Council of War. Was this something unplanned?

Worse—was there no formal plan at all? Was each of

them to contribute spontaneous bits of malice as and when inspiration occurred to them?

That way lay chaos. But, knowing my family, it was only too possible.

"I can't stand here arguing with you all day—" Abruptly Mrs. Keyes ended the impasse. "You just ask that child, that's all. You'll find out—" She turned and retreated to the kitchen.

"Oh dear!" Aunt Maddy looked after her, distressed. "I'm afraid she's right, you know. Not about Lynnie. But that *she* didn't do it."

Our eyes met again, acknowledging the unspoken question.

"Well . . ." Aunt Maddy sighed and absently shook the plastic container in her hand. The pellets rattled.

Death rattle. The thought came unbidden and I tried to dismiss it. There was no certainty that the pellets would have killed Wanda-Lu had she been incautious enough to swallow any. They were only known to be deadly to slugs.

I could not pretend, however—even to myself—that they would have done her any good.

"I'll throw these away," Aunt Maddy said decisively, slipping the container into the pocket of her cardigan. "And we'll put aspirins on the shopping list—" She paused thoughtfully. "A box of foil-wrapped aspirins, I think. Then there can't be any possibility of another . . . mistake."

Not about aspirins.

"And perhaps—" Aunt Maddy followed my train of thought—"We ought to have a word with your cousins."

* * *

By late afternoon, the guests from town had begun to arrive for the official birthday party. I greeted Uncle Wilmer's agent, publishers, radio and television colleagues and a nondescript little man who seemed always to be around. I suspected him of having pretensions toward being Uncle Wilmer's official biographer. Well, he'd collect material for a sensational chapter tonight.

Uncle Wilmer and Wanda-Lu were lurking upstairs. With his usual fine sense of drama, Uncle Wilmer wanted to spring his surprise at the outset of the party. He planned to descend the staircase, leading his bride, and present her to the guests assembled at the foot of the stairs. Before the gasps of astonishment and the applause had had time to die away, the family had orders to let fly with the champagne corks and pass among the guests pouring champagne for a gala toast, thus presenting a festive and united front—in public. I hoped the applause would be loud enough to cover the gnashing of teeth.

There was no doubt, however, that the total effect would be just what Uncle Wilmer planned. The emphasis would be shifted from the passage of years to romance and new beginnings. From being an ageing pundit, he would become a fairly dashing—perhaps rakish—figure. His audience would lap it up.

Inevitably, the Press must follow...

"I can handle it alone, I tell you—" I caught Toy Boy on the downstairs phone. "I've already got most of the pictures. I can do the story—"

I tapped him on the shoulder. He shrugged me off irritably, without looking around. I tapped again.

"Just a minute, Tom, I've got a bit of interference on this end." He clamped a hand over the mouthpiece and swung around. "Now listen, Tamar, I've told you—Oh!"

"That's right," I said. "It isn't Tamar."

"Oh." Losing interest, he turned back to the phone. "Look, Tom, send a messenger down to collect the film, right? I'll phone in the text after the party. The pictures are the main thing. I've got some great ones—"

I tried another tap and left my hand on his shoulder.

"Look—!" He swung around savagely. "Someone's got to do it. You'd rather have me than the rest of them swarming all over, wouldn't you?"

I nodded. "But—"

"*Don't* let me break anything up!" My hand was unceremoniously lifted from Toy Boy's shoulder and Tamar stood there, glaring at me.

"You needn't worry," I said. "I wasn't poaching." I wouldn't have him gift-wrapped, but I could hardly add that with him still standing there.

Snarling with exasperation, Toy Boy turned his back on both of us, finished his conversation in rapid *sotto voce*, and slammed down the receiver.

"That's better," Tamar said. "I want to have a little talk with you. *If* you can possibly spare me a moment, that is. I know how busy you are lately."

I winced and moved away to escape getting caught in the crossfire. I sympathized—up to a point. But if Tamar was going to interrupt every time Toy Boy tried to talk to a girl of his own age, she'd have a lifetime's work cut out for her.

Of course, it was unlikely that this little liaison would last a lifetime. None of the others had.

"As a matter of fact, I *am* busy." There was more than

a trace of tedium in the look Toy Boy gave her. "I'm working."

"That's the trouble," Tamar pouted. "I invited you down here for a holiday. I wanted you to meet my family and—"

The snort produced by Toy Boy was worthy of Aunt Maddy. Tamar wasn't fooling him. She had brought him down here to flaunt in front of her family, hoping to shock and upset them. She was in a fury because, after the initial impact, it hadn't worked out that way. She had been upstaged by her own father and now her lover was ignoring her, more interested in the story he had stumbled upon than in her. A girlfriend was only a girlfriend, but an exclusive like this about a newly-created Knight was money in the bank.

"I thought we might go down to the pub for a drink," Tamar said. "Escape from all these awful people for a while before the party starts."

There would be no escape then. Uncle Wilmer would consider it a major defection if all his family were not present for his big moment.

"Listen—" Carelessly, Toy Boy betrayed that he had not been listening and had missed the entire point. "I'm too busy right now. You go ahead and perhaps I'll—"

In a swift, totally unexpected movement, Tamar drew back her hand and swung at him. She hit him so hard he staggered, shaking his head groggily.

I didn't want to see what his response would be. I was close to the front door and I slipped through it and went around into the garden.

* * *

Cromwell glared down from his branch and cursed pungently. He was holding me personally responsible for this new invision of undesirables.

"You're one of the family, all right," I told him. "You're bad-tempered enough."

He let me know it. I moved away from his ear-splitting blast . . .

"That's right—" Godfrey was talking to one of the television people. "We're just one big happy family. United we stand—"

I retreated hastily, wondering if the woman had noticed the grim glint in his eye and the set of his jaw. I didn't want to get involved in that one, either.

The very fact that Godfrey had been moved to utter the declaration—obviously in response to some remark of hers—showed that rumors were already starting to circulate.

I sought refuge in the herb garden. For a moment, I thought I had found sanctuary; then I realized that I was not alone.

"Tell me—" Uncle Wilmer's literary agent advanced on me, eyes gleaming—"is it true that Sir Wilmer has adopted an American teeny-bopper?"

"Why don't you ask him yourself?" I hurled over my shoulder as I dived for the shelter of the kitchen.

"Manners of a pig!" Mrs. Keyes snapped as the door slammed shut behind me.

By this time, I was in as bad a temper as Cromwell. Only self-preservation kept me from telling her to shut up. The buffet was coming along nicely and she'd storm out leaving whatever was in the oven to burn if anyone upset her further.

As it was, there was something strange about the

kitchen. I didn't dare linger and look around—that could be construed as provocation in the mood Mrs. Keyes was in.

I did notice, on my way through, that she was working on the birthday cake with a large bowl of white icing, presumably to try to make it look more like a wedding cake. The carefully traced birthday message had been obliterated under a fluffy white cloud and the seven large candles—one for each decade—had been tactfully removed.

Then I was safely on the other side of the green baize door. Or was it so safe?

"Pippa—" Jennifer bore down on me with a frown that portended no good—"have you seen—?"

"Sorry." I darted past her and up the stairs. "Haven't seen anyone and haven't a minute to talk. It's time to get changed for the party."

It was, as someone remarked later, the greatest staircase scene since Rhett Butler swept Scarlett O'Hara into his arms and carried her up to the bedroom.

Except that, in this case, the happy couple were coming downstairs. Wanda-Lu's Southern accent might have contributed to the resemblance, but there the similarity ended.

For one thing, she could hardly get a word in edgeways. For another, as the same person also remarked, Wanda-Lu looked robust enough to carry Sir Wilmer, rather than the other way around.

But such carping didn't surface until the later editions of the next day's papers. For tonight, Uncle Sir Wilmer had achieved his objective and was well pleased with the sensation he had created.

"Of course we were surprised—" Godfrey admitted between clenched teeth, recklessly splashing champagne into a proffered glass—"but delighted."

"Of course," the recipient of the champagne cooed, not believing it for a moment. "So nice for you to have a stepmo—I mean, for your father to have a . . . companion."

Godfrey turned away abruptly. He nearly collided with me. Our champagne bottles clinked together.

"Steady on," I warned. Toy Boy was aiming his camera in our direction. We instantly flashed rapturous smiles as Uncle Wilmer moved through the throng, leading his bride into the drawing room.

We topped up any glass that wasn't brimming over as the guests crowded past us to follow the happy couple. It was simply unfortunate that Toy Boy caught us with empty bottles looking at each other with distinctly jaded expressions.

"I can't stand much more of this," Godfrey groaned.

"The worst is over now." I really believed it. "The big secret is out, so that will end the rumors. There'll still be some pointed remarks, of course—"

Godfrey groaned again.

"But we just have to get through the rest of the evening," I finished cheerfully, heading for the kitchen and replenishments. "The party will break up about midnight because the guests have to get back to town. They'll have a delicious day tomorrow spreading the scandalous news. And from then on, it's Uncle Wilmer who'll have to bear the brunt of it."

We collected and opened fresh bottles of champagne and brought them to the drawing room where Uncle Wilmer was ensconced on the sofa with Wanda-Lu, beginning to open his presents.

It was an awkward moment—for the guests, if not for Uncle Wilmer. They had brought birthday presents and it now turned out that they should have brought wedding gifts.

A few smug faces betrayed that an occasional contribution could double as both.

"How beautiful!" Wanda-Lu exclaimed as Uncle Wilmer passed a solid silver rose bowl to her. Its donor smiled and nodded wisely, as though she had possessed inside information.

A first edition and a small Victorian oil painting also did double duty and were passed to Wanda-Lu as though they had, indeed, been intended to celebrate the wedding.

But the presents from the family gave the game away, proving that Uncle Wilmer's nearest and dearest had not been forewarned in any way.

The large canister of specially blended pipe tobacco and the length of cashmere suiting could only have been intended as very personal birthday presents. There was a ripple of amusement through the room as the guests realized how thoroughly Uncle Wilmer had surprised, not just them, but his own family.

Several white envelopes, not attached to any presents, were scattered through the diminishing pile on the coffee table. They appeared to be last-minute additions, obviously hastily obtained wedding congratulation cards, possibly containing promises of future, more suitable, gifts.

"How splendid, Lynette. Thank you." In response to urgent signals, Uncle Wilmer opened Lynette's present. "Just what I need—a new umbrella." Blushing, Lynette advanced to be kissed and fussed over. Now Davina could unobtrusively whisk her away and put her to bed while the party continued for the adults.

"I learned a poem—" Lynette began shyly.

"Tell me tomorrow, dear." Uncle Wilmer passed her along to Wanda-Lu. He was the star of tonight's show, after all, and he wasn't going to share the spotlight.

Lynette pushed herself away from Wanda-Lu, lower lip trembling. She was not ordinarily a troublesome child, but it appeared that she was now on the verge of a tearful tantrum. Uncle Wilmer would not be pleased.

"Come, Lynette—" Davina stepped forward, reading the signs expertly and trying to avoid the threatened trouble. "It's time we went home. It's well past your bedtime. You can come over tomorrow and—" she shot a meaningful glance at Uncle Wilmer, who was doing his best to ignore the situation—"and have the birthday boy all to yourself."

It was as close to sarcasm as I had ever heard Davina get in public. I glanced at her, startled. No one else appeared to have noticed, although a faint frown crossed Uncle Wilmer's forehead.

He masked it quickly, passing a gift-wrapped parcel to Wanda-Lu to open, while he opened one of the white envelopes scattered through the pile.

I was watching Davina coax Lynette out of the room and so I missed the first expression that crossed Uncle Wilmer's face. I turned as I heard the choked exclamation and was in time to see him clutch at his heart.

The guests surged forward, led by the doctor, who immediately began to urge the others to step back and give the victim air.

"Oh, Wilmer, darlin'—" Wanda-Lu's voice rose above the others as she fought to control her frightened sobs.

I rushed to Uncle Wilmer, pushing aside the guests in my way. Already some of them had retreated to the far side of the room wearing the bemused expressions of people planning their excuses for early departure. The sooner all of them left, the better.

"No, no—I'm all right," Uncle Wilmer said testily. "Quite all right!" He crumpled the envelope he was still holding and thrust it into his pocket. "It was just a twinge."

Aunt Maddy's sharp sniff punctuated his remarks. Aunt Flora's icy stare at Wanda-Lu implied that *she* knew the reasons why an elderly man should be having sudden twinges.

It was rather surprising that Davina had not returned to the room when the commotion started. Perhaps she had not heard it. Perhaps she thought it would be best if Lynette did not witness what might have turned out to be a traumatic scene. Or perhaps it had finally been brought home to her that whatever happened to Uncle Wilmer was no longer any of her business.

"I . . . er . . . ought to be getting along now," a voice announced from the doorway. "If everything is all right, that is. It's a long drive back to London."

There were murmurs of agreement. Even the media people were ready to leave now that it appeared that the evening was not to be marked by high drama. Since Uncle Wilmer had not dropped dead on the spot, it was clear that he was going to last for some while yet. A pertinent—or impertinent—paragraph was all that a twinge in an average bridegroom rated. There would be no banner headlines made tonight.

"Maybe it *is* time for the party to break up—" Wanda-Lu was not prepared to urge the guests to stand upon the order of their going. "We're all kinda tired and jet-lagged."

Uncle Wilmer, still a choleric color, surprisingly nodded agreement. He insisted on standing by the doorway, however, and saying goodnight to everyone. The guests were obviously nervous and the goodnights were not prolonged.

And yet, there was just something slightly wrong about Uncle Wilmer's attitude.

As the last guest exited, my mind replayed the earlier scene.

It occurred to me that Uncle Wilmer's cry might not have been one of pain so much as one of outrage.

CHAPTER 14

I WAS NOT THE ONLY ONE TO SPEND A RESTLESS NIGHT. Waking at intervals, I heard footsteps in both the upper and lower hallways. Rising once, I encountered Aunt Maddy at the bathroom door. She was not quite awake, either.

Behind closed doors, one of the dogs barked. Aunt

Maddy looked around vaguely and gave a disparaging sniff. Like the rest of the regular occupants of the house, she really preferred Cromwell.

"I hope that doesn't start the others off," she said. "They'll rouse the whole house."

"Uncle Wilmer wouldn't like it," I agreed.

Aunt Maddy sniffed again, conveying that Uncle Wilmer's likes and dislikes were no longer of paramount importance to her, and headed back to her room.

The barking was abruptly hushed, as though by a bad-tempered slap. So someone else was awake—or had been awakened by the noise.

Outside, from his tree-top, Cromwell gave one faint complaining cry, almost a reflex action as he stirred in his sleep.

"Not to worry, old boy," I murmured, although he could not hear me. "It's almost over now. Most of them will be leaving tomorrow—or today—and the place will be yours again . . ."

I thought I was the first one up in the morning but, when I got downstairs, Aunt Maddy was padding about the kitchen, emitting sniffs of suspicion.

"Mrs. Keyes is up to something," she greeted me. "Just look!" She indicated the kitchen table, where sugar bowl, jam-jar and cornflakes packet clustered together neatly in the center, ready for breakfast.

"You're right—that's positively unnatural." I moved closer. "What's in them?"

"Sugar, jam and cornflakes," Aunt Maddy said. "I thought at first it was some sort of booby-trap, but they're all just what they're supposed to be. Do you suppose she's turning over a new leaf?"

"I wouldn't count on it. As soon as she's over her scare about the slug pellets, she'll probably lapse back into her old ways."

"I hope so." Aunt Maddy sighed. "I've just learned where to look for things. If she starts putting them in their proper places, I'll never find anything again."

"She'll get over it." I sat down and shook cornflakes into my bowl abstractedly. There seemed to be a peculiar noise in my ears, something just barely audible. I stopped rustling the cornflakes to listen.

It wasn't Cromwell. I was familiar with every pitch and variation of his voice. Besides, he was already wailing in the background. This was more of a faint spasmodic whimper.

I crossed to the back door and opened it. Lynette, seated on the back step, raised tear-drenched eyes to me. Cromwell wailed again and she looked towards him, a sob escaping her.

"Don't worry, Lynnie," I said consolingly. "Cromwell's all right. He'll come down when all the guests have gone and then you can play together."

She turned back to me, shaking her head. It wasn't Cromwell's plight she was worried about. She snuffled again.

"Well, what's the matter, then, Lynnie?"

She took a deep choking breath and said the words guaranteed to produce that sinking sensation in the heart and stomach of any neighbor:

"Mummy won't wake up."

There was a strangulated gasp behind me and Aunt Maddy darted forward to swoop on Lynette.

"Come and have breakfast, Lynnie. You must be hungry." She pulled the child to her feet and hurled directions *sotto voce* over her shoulder to me.

"Wake Jennifer—she can see to Lynette. You and I will go next door and investigate." She added, without any great conviction, "Davina has probably taken a sleeping pill. It's most inconsiderate of her to frighten Lynette like this."

"Oh, Lor'!" Jennifer said, on a note of rising panic. "I don't like the sound of that!" She scrambled into her clothes and we hurried downstairs, slowing our steps as we reached the kitchen in order to make an ordinary entrance.

"Lynette is having cornflakes," Aunt Maddy greeted us. "And we've made a cup of coffee to take over to her Mummy to help her wake up."

Lynette nodded gravely and spooned far too much sugar into the cup Aunt Maddy had indicated. She was no longer so worried; the grown-ups had the problem under control now and had provided the solution. Of course, a nice hot cup of coffee brought to Mummy in bed would wake her up.

I only hoped so.

"Jennifer will find you a banana to slice over your cornflakes," Aunt Maddy said firmly. "And Pippa and I will go over and bring Mummy her coffee."

Lynette nodded again and gave Jennifer a welcoming smile.

"Now then, young Lynnie," Jennifer said, a shade too heartily, "let's find those bananas." She started for the cabinet under the sink.

"They're in the fruit bowl in the larder," Aunt Maddy said.

"They are?" Jennifer stopped short in amazement. "What on earth is happening?"

"That's what we're going to find out." Aunt Maddy picked up the cup of coffee and moved to the back door. "Come along, Pippa—"

I smiled reassuringly at Lynette and followed Aunt Maddy out and across the yard. Above us, Cromwell howled mournfully.

"I hope he doesn't know something we don't know," I said.

"Nonsense!" Aunt Maddy snapped. "Only dogs are supposed to howl when their masters die. Wilmer is perfectly all right and Cromwell never gave a tinker's curse about Davina. He's just being melodramatic again. There are times when I'd like to strangle that creature!"

The over-reaction was a measure of her concern. I didn't try to make any further sprightly conversation. In silence, we entered Davina's kitchen and Aunt Maddy deposited the camouflaging cup of coffee on the draining board.

"If it's needed, you can go down for it," she said. I realized that she had already formed her own opinion of what might have happened.

She hesitated then, making strangely ineffectual little gestures towards the plate rack, as though she would like to polish the two whisky glasses, to put away the cutlery— to do anything except lead the way upstairs to Davina's bedroom.

I waited.

"Well—" She sighed deeply. "I suppose we might as

well go up. Although what we'll say if Davina wakes up and finds us staring at her. . ." She let the thought trail off, she didn't really believe it. By this time, neither did I.

I caught myself echoing Aunt Maddy's sighs as we climbed the stairs and closed my mouth firmly. That was a habit I didn't want to pick up. At the same time, I was conscious of the pounding of my heart and realized that the sighing had brought some relief from tension.

Aunt Maddy hesitated again at the top of the stairs. It was most unlike her.

"To the left," I said loudly, although she knew her way about the house as well as I did. I still held the vague hope that Davina might be awakened by our voices and we would find her sitting up in bed—puzzled and perhaps indignant, but sitting up—when we entered.

"I know." Aunt Maddy shot me a sharp, almost mocking, glance, as though she had read my thoughts.

We proceeded without undue haste, reluctant to reach our goal. Lynette was a perspicacious—and persistent—child. If she had not been able to rouse her mother, it was highly unlikely that we could.

"We ought to call the doctor," I said.

"We can't do that until we've checked for ourselves," Aunt Maddy said.

We stopped at the bedroom door. It was slightly ajar, probably the way Lynette had left it. There was no sound of movement from within the room.

"Davina—" Aunt Maddy called out formally. "Davina—are you awake?"

There was no answer.

"Davina!" For good measure, Aunt Maddy rapped sharply on the door before pushing it open. "Davina—"

Davina lay motionless on her back. The bedclothes around her were disturbed, showing that Lynette had tried to shake her back to consciousness. There was something awful about her utter stillness—and the gleam of white eyeball between partly-open eyelids.

"Oh heavens!" Aunt Maddy sighed. "I was hoping it couldn't be true."

"We both were." I advanced with her to stand beside the bed.

"Do you think it could be a coma?" I grasped at one last straw.

Aunt Maddy steeled herself visibly and reached out for Davina's wrist. She paled as her fingers curled around it, but held on long enough to make certain.

"There's no pulse," she reported. "And . . . and she's terribly cold." She took a deep breath and drew back, instinctively wiping her hand on her skirt.

"A mirror—" I stumbled to the dressing-table and snatched up the hand mirror, knowing it would only confirm what we already knew.

My hand was unsteady as I held the mirror above Davina's parted lips, but it didn't matter. The mirror failed to cloud even slightly. There was no breath in that rapidly-chilling body.

Aunt Maddy and I sighed in unison.

"*Now*—" Aunt Maddy looked around the room. Her gaze lingered on the bedside table, the few drops of water in the water glass, the empty pill bottle. She shook her head sadly.

"*Now* we'd better call the doctor."

* * *

Everyone was awake and stirring when we returned. By contrast, our house seemed to vibrate with movement. Having fed Lynette, Jennifer was now feeding all three dogs in the kitchen. Lynette was helping, intent on her task.

Jennifer looked up when we entered and raised her eyebrows in silent inquiry. The look on our faces must have answered her; she let her eyebrows fall back into place.

"Mummy?" Lynette heard the click of the latch and turned to the door in sudden hope.

"Mummy is . . . still resting," Aunt Maddy said.

Lynette's face fell.

"Oh God!" Jennifer choked, turning away.

"Pippa, why don't you take Lynnie down to the village and buy her an ice cream?" Aunt Maddy suggested. *So that she'll be safely out of the way when the authorities arrive.*

"What a good idea!" I would be just as happy to get away myself. "Come along, Lynnie—" I held out my hand.

Lynette hung back, sensing something wrong. I wondered who would have to be the one to break it to her eventually. I didn't want to.

Abruptly, I remembered the day they had told me about my parents' fatal accident. The long wait on the bench outside the Headmistress's study; the rumble of conversation, too muffled to be understood, from behind closed doors. Above all, the overpowering feeling of guilt and impending punishment. Children can always dredge up a dozen small peccadilloes and infractions of rules to feel guilty about. When nemesis descends, it brings no great surprise, just the question of which particular misdemeanor has been discovered. Then the door had opened and I had glimpsed Uncle Wilmer, grave and concerned, waiting to tell me that I would always have a home with him.

"Come, Lynette—" I had a fellow-feeling for her. "You can bring the dogs, if you like," I added. "They could do with a run."

As I had hoped, this distracted her. By the time she had found the leashes and harnessed the dogs, the day had acquired a semblance of normality for her and she was content to leave larger worries to the adults who were already beginning to huddle together, whispering mysteriously.

"Are we ready?" I accepted Rex's leash, feeling a sedate senior dog was as much as I could cope with, while Frou-Frou and Nell frisked around Lynette, anxious to be off.

We were almost to the gate when I saw Toy Boy, one camera around his neck and the other at the ready, descend the stairs from his room over the garage and head purposefully for the cottage next door.

"Here—hold this!" I thrust Rex's leash into Lynette's hand and sped after Toy Boy.

"Stop right there!" I grabbed him by the arm holding the camera and he flinched.

"Oh, it's you." He relaxed. "What's the matter?"

"Where are you going?"

"Oh, er, I was just wandering around." His eyes shifted guiltily. "Where are *you* going?"

"To the village with Lynette." I decided to put a spoke in his wheel. "Why don't you come along?"

"Too busy," he said quickly, before realizing it was the wrong thing to say. "I mean—"

"You mean you've been talking to Tamar and she's told you about Davina. Well, you can forget it! It's just not on! No pictures over there. Try it, and I'll smash your camera myself!"

"Take it easy." He cradled his camera protectively. "I'm only trying to earn a living."

"There must be a better way—"

But he had stopped listening to me. Looking beyond me, he had spotted Lynette. He moved towards her, smiling falsely.

"Aren't you looking pretty this morning? Would you like your picture taken?"

Lynette smiled radiantly as the camera clicked. It clicked several more times before it was lowered, Toy Boy moving rapidly, crouching and shifting to different angles to make up for Lynette's lack of movement.

"That's fine." His heartiness did not quite mask his dissatisfaction. "Now can we try a few more in a different pose? Can you look serious for a minute? Sad, even?"

I gave him a push that sent him flying. He retained his cameras with difficulty, staggered and turned to me indignantly.

"Why did you—?" He broke off as I gestured fiercely towards Lynette, who had abandoned all semblance of posing and was watching us with open-mouthed fascination.

"You mean she doesn't know yet? But I thought she

dis—'' I gave him another push to take us both out of Lynette's hearing.

"You didn't think at all!" I blazed. "You have a camera instead of a brain!"

"Look, I apologize—"

"She *doesn't* know yet. We're trying to keep her happy for just a few more hours."

Already, in the background, Lynette was beginning to look concerned. It was always something to worry about when adults began whispering together urgently and casting sidelong glances in your direction.

"We'd better get back to her," I told Toy Boy. "She'll begin suspecting something. I want to get her clear of the house before the doctor and ambulance get here."

"I'll walk you part of the way," he said. It was clear that he intended to turn back and get his pictures no matter what I said. "I'd like to get a few more shots of the kid. Don't worry—I won't say anything to give the game away."

"You'd better not," I warned. Poor Lynette. At least, I had had the consolation of knowing that my parents had not intended to leave me. It had been a tragic, appalling traffic accident, but it had been an accident.

How could Davina have done it? No matter how wounded her pride, no matter how much a fool she might have felt, how could she have taken those sleeping pills and drifted away, leaving her child alone and defenceless in the world?

"Let Lynette be as happy as she can for the next few hours," I said. "She'll have to live with this for the rest of her life."

CHAPTER 15

"IT'S DISGUSTING!" AUNT FLORA TRUMPETED. "INDEcent! The old ram ought to be shot!"

"Please, Flora," Aunt Maddy said wearily. "It isn't Will's fault that the woman was so unbalanced she killed herself." She did not sound entirely convinced.

"Tell *that* to the newspapers!"

Aunt Maddy moaned softly.

"They'll turn this into a Roman Holiday," Aunt Flora continued relentlessly. "None of us will ever live it down!"

It was all too probable that she was right. Sir Wilmer Creighleigh as *homme fatale* would be too much for any newspaper to resist. The suicide of his next-door neighbor and "close friend" following immediately upon his return from America with a "teen-aged bride" was certain to make headlines.

I had to admit to myself that, were I not personally involved, I'd buy the newspapers myself to get all the juicy bits of scandalous innuendo. But it wasn't so funny when you were caught up in the middle of it and knew all the people concerned. And were face to face with all the problems entailed.

For a start, there was Toy Boy out prowling with his precious cameras at the ready and Tamar barely speaking to him because he was taking full advantage of a situation she herself had pitched him into. But that was a petty, easily-solved problem. Sooner or later they would have to return to London, whether together or separately remained to be seen. It was possible that Toy Boy's behavior was precipitating the inevitable final break-up.

Wanda-Lu and Uncle Wilmer were closeted in the library with Jarvis Fortescue and the Triffid, sorting out the easiest of their problems: the financial ones. I knew, from what Wanda-Lu had let slip, that they would be dealing with joint bank accounts, financial investments and new wills—not that Wanda-Lu was old enough ever to have thought about making a will before.

"At least," Aunt Flora said, on a note of grudging thankfulness, "the woman didn't leave a letter. Unless—" a new and frightening thought occurred to her—"it's in the post, waiting to be delivered."

As one, we all looked towards the front door.

"There was nothing in the first post," I said uncertainly.

"Well, there wouldn't be, would there?" Jennifer frowned. "If she posted it after she left the party last night, it wouldn't be collected until this morning. It might arrive this afternoon, but more probably tomorrow."

"Unless it went second-class." Aunt Flora seemed intent upon being the voice of doom. "In that case, it could take anywhere up to a week or more."

We shared a communal shudder at the threat hanging over us for that length of time.

"This is just awful!" Tamar burst out. "How *could* Davina have done such a thing to us?"

"*You* should talk!" It had been most unwise of Tamar to draw Aunt Flora's fire. "*You* with your—your—living-in *spy*!"

"Now just a minute—"

"It's quite bad enough—" Aunt Flora was not to be halted—"that you should choose to—to *disport* yourself with the most unsuitable partners you can find. But to bring them down *here* and turn them loose to spy on the family and photograph us for the scandal sheets—"

"Hold hard, Aunt Flora." Godfrey obviously felt that he should protest. "That's not entirely fair. Tamar wasn't to know there'd be anything sensational down here to photograph. No one ever expected Father to bring home a bride—and such a young one, at that."

"Yes," Aunt Flora said darkly, "it *all* comes back to Wilmer."

"What's done is done," Aunt Maddy said.

"More's the pity! If you ask me—" Aunt Flora stopped short.

The problem none of us wanted to think about was standing in the doorway.

"Hello, Lynnie," Aunt Maddy said. "Have you finished your jigsaw puzzle already?"

Lynette shook her head and sidled into the room. We had settled her upstairs in my study with a simplified jigsaw puzzle. It had been too much to hope that she would stay there and play with it.

"Thank you," she said politely. "I've had a very nice visit, but I want to go home now. Mummy will be looking for me."

The silence lengthened as we waited, each hoping someone else would be the one to speak.

"Please—" Lynette was not a stupid child, but she was out of her depth and knew it. The mere fact that she was asking permission to go home when she had always run carelessly back and forth between the two houses betrayed that she knew something was very wrong. "Please, I want to go home. My Mummy will be worried."

"You don't want to go yet, Lynnie," Jennifer said. "We were hoping you'd stay a while longer. Your . . . your Mummy wouldn't mind. And I was counting on you to take the dogs for a nice long walk this afternoon."

The blandishment failed, as we had known it must.

"I can come back later." That was the flaw, it was not as if Lynette lived miles away. Politely stubborn, she held to her point. "I want to go home now."

We had kept her out of the way while the doctor, the ambulance and, inevitably, the police had gone in and out of the house next door. It was horrifying and strange to us, but just a matter of routine to them; the well-worn path officialdom must travel when a citizen in previously good health is found dead. We had answered their simple preliminary questions about how we had come to discover what had happened and they had agreed that this was not the right time to question Lynette. It seemed that they were disconcerted by the realization that not only had she not been told yet that her mother was dead, but that she now had no guardian to be present when they spoke to her. However, they were relieved to learn that we were willing to look after Lynette until a relative could be located. The local constabulary did not have the facilities to board a bereft five-year-old and they were pleased to take advantage of our offer to keep her.

I now began to see why they had been so quietly relieved. They had known from experience that this moment must come—and they had not wanted to be the ones who tried to explain just why she couldn't go home again.

"Please." Lynette was trying to be a good little girl, struggling to be polite, but she was on the verge of tears.

With a muffled exclamation, Godfrey got up abruptly and crossed over to the window, dissociating himself from the problem.

"All right, Lynnie." Aunt Maddy sighed deeply. "We'll go over to your house." She looked at the rest of us, almost apologetically. "I'll have to pack some things for her, anyway," she said.

"I can't understand why you're making such heavy weather of this," Uncle Wilmer said. "I can't see any difficulty—"

He probably could not. He had been shocked and perhaps saddened by the news about Davina, but he was cushioned by his new interest in life: Wanda-Lu. Off with the old, on with the new.

They had joined us in the drawing room, the financial conference over. Jarvis Fortescue and the Triffid had dashed through the room ahead of us, expressions of relief on their faces as they headed for freedom. That should have warned us of the mood Uncle Wilmer was in.

"Do be sensible, Wilmer," Aunt Flora said. "The child can't stay here indefinitely."

"I don't see why not. There's plenty of room and it will be rather pleasant to put the old nursery to its proper use." He failed to notice that his bride was no more enthusiastic about his idea than the rest of the family.

"I've got a few plans of my own for that nursery, Wilmer darlin'." There was a trace of steel in Wanda-Lu's voice. It was an interesting portent that Uncle Wilmer was not going to have it all his own way in the future.

Neither of them seemed to notice—or care—that they would be effectively dispossessing me. True, I'd still have my bedroom, but the adjoining study had meant a lot of extra comfort and space for me. I did not like the idea of losing it.

"There's plenty of room," Uncle Wilmer repeated. "Lynette knows us and loves us. Oh, she'll miss her mother, of course—" He tossed it off with bloodless abandon. "But she'll soon settle down. It will be much easier for her than being sent away to live among strangers in a strange place. It's the ideal solution."

He was the only one who thought this. There was a careful silence.

"Wilmer darlin'—" Wanda-Lu's drawl was becoming more pronounced—"Ah don't think you've considered the long-term consequences. Ah mean—" her voice sharpened—"it could get awfully awkward in the future."

"I don't see why." Uncle Wilmer frowned; he was not accustomed to having his wishes questioned. The others remained very quiet. It was a revelation to them that the new Lady Creighleigh might not be the obliging cipher everyone had thought her. She had a will of her own and she did not seem overly concerned about letting it be known.

"Your *wife*—" Aunt Flora spoke with delicate emphasis—

"is right, Wilmer. This isn't something you can rush into without thinking about the future. It may be all right to keep Lynette for a few days, or perhaps a few weeks—"

"I see no reason why she shouldn't remain permanently. It wouldn't be the first time we've taken a child into the house and—" he sent me a conspiratorial smile, trying to enlist me on his side—"and it didn't work out too badly, did it?"

"Pippa is our cousin." Jennifer could not let that pass. "Lynette is a sweet child, but she's nothing to us."

"Nothing to you!" Uncle Wilmer was shocked. "That's a very harsh attitude. I'm surprised at you, Jennifer. Lynette is a child in trouble. Left alone—"

"Are you thinking of adopting her?" Aunt Flora demanded.

"I wouldn't rule out the possibility—"

"Wilmer darlin', ah *do* think that's a matter for private discussion, don't you?"

"I quite agree with your *wife*," Aunt Flora said, not disdaining an unlikely ally. "After all, you may start this with the best of intentions but . . . if anything should happen to you, then Wanda-Lu will be left with the responsibility for a child she's barely met."

Only Aunt Flora would have had the audacity to come right out with the statement, true though it was. Uncle Wilmer's face became so choleric that I was afraid he was going to have a seizure on the spot.

"Anyhow," Wanda-Lu said hastily, "I'm sure it wouldn't be so easy, Wilmer. There are all sorts of laws. You can't just take over a little girl the way you would a stray cat. She must have relatives of her own. Her Daddy would surely have something to say about it."

The thought did not appear to calm Uncle Wilmer. He opened and closed his mouth several times, but no words came out. I knew he hated to be crossed, but this was the first time I had seen it leave him speechless. Of course, Wanda-Lu was quite right—and that didn't help matters any. I made a mental bet that, as soon as they were alone, the lovebirds were going to have a monumental row.

"The girl is quite right, Wilmer," Aunt Flora said with relief. "Davina's ex-husband must be notified immediately. Does anyone know where he can be reached?"

Silence answered her. Davina had already been divorced and Lynette a small baby when they took up residence next door. We had never heard her speak of her ex-husband, which was not unusual in such cases. None of us had ever been curious enough to inquire about him. It was Davina's business. If she wanted to close the door on what had obviously been an unhappy episode, and start anew, that was her privilege.

"Surely the police will take care of that," Jennifer said sensibly. "They must have ways of tracing him."

"He won't want Lynette," Uncle Wilmer said. "In all these years, he's never come near her. He'd be a total stranger to her."

"That may have been Davina's fault. It's a completely different situation now that she's dead. The man has a right to a say in his child's future." Aunt Flora had one last triumphant thought. "Perhaps there's a grandmother who could take her, if he hasn't married again."

"It would be quite ridiculous," Uncle Wilmer said coldly, "to remove the child from an environment in which she is happy and hand her over to strangers."

"But, Wilmer darlin'—" Wanda-Lu was looking at him as though he were a stranger himself; this was obviously her first view of the autocratic, unreasonable side of him; the honeymoon was over. "The child's father has *some* rights. He's probably quite a nice man, even though he didn't get along with her mother. Ah'm sure little Lynette will adjust and settle down with him and be happy."

"It's out of the question!" Uncle Wilmer snapped. "She'd never be happy!"

They glared at each other. Any of us could have told Wanda-Lu that Uncle Wilmer was not susceptible to the voice of sweet reason in his current mood. However, she was discovering the fact for herself.

"Nevertheless, the law will have something to say on the subject." Aunt Flora sounded grateful for that. "The decision is out of our hands."

"We'll see about that," Uncle Wilmer snapped. He turned to me. "Get me Trifflin!"

I was glad to get out of the room. I was not so glad to find the Triffid and Toy Boy together in the garden and deep in conversation. At the same time, I recognized that my attitude was not entirely rational. One could hardly issue an edict forbidding guests to gossip about the circumstances in which they found themselves—however much one might like to.

They stopped talking abruptly as they noticed me approaching and assumed the unconcerned expressions of men with extremely guilty consciences. They had been discussing the family, all right.

Perhaps Toy Boy couldn't be blamed so much. He had

been dragged into the long weekend as a more or less innocent bystander; but the Triffid was junior partner in the law firm handling Uncle Wilmer's business. As such, we had a right to expect professional discretion from him.

"Sir Wilmer would like to speak to you," I informed him icily.

"That sounds as though you wouldn't," he said, not quite as easily as he had obviously hoped. He was getting the message. "Why so formal?"

"They're barking mad, I tell you." Toy Boy reiterated his opinion. "Every last one of them."

"I'm sure Tamar will be interested to know your diagnosis," I said. "If *she's* still speaking to *you*, that is."

"Funny you should mention that." It obviously didn't bother him. "The last I heard, she said she never wanted to speak to me again. She gets that way, you know."

I knew, but I wasn't going to admit it. Our best hope now was that he'd take Tamar's decision as final and go away—taking his cameras with him.

Meanwhile, the Triffid seemed to have grown roots, like his namesake.

"Sir Wilmer is waiting for you," I prodded.

"Let him wait." Toy Boy continued to give unasked advice. "It will do him a world of good. Too many people jumping every time he snaps his fingers, that's his trouble."

"Perhaps they want to remain employed," I said pointedly.

The Triffid stirred uneasily, as though envisaging his father's reaction if he lost the firm such a prominent client. "Er," he said, "perhaps I ought to go in and see what Sir Wilmer wants.'' He began moving reluctantly towards the house.

''I should think so!'' I closed in behind him like a sheepdog, lest he stray off course.

Then Lynette came through the gap in the hedge, followed by Aunt Maddy, carrying the case. The look on Aunt Maddy's face stopped me in my tracks.

''It's no use, Pippa.'' Aunt Maddy came up to me, heedless of spectators. ''I don't believe it!''

''Lynette,'' I said hastily, ''why don't you go over and see if you can coax Cromwell out of the tree. He must be hungry by now. He ought to be ready to come down for some food.''

Lynette's face was blotched and tear-stained. She looked at me and turned away without a word. We weren't fooling her, we were going to say something we didn't want her to hear, but she didn't care any more.

''I don't believe it!'' Aunt Maddy said again. ''I had a chance to look around while I was collecting Lynette's things, and nothing will convince me that it's true. Davina cared too much about Lynette—she'd never have deserted her like that. It must have been an accident. Perhaps the wrong pills got into the wrong bottle again. But Davina didn't commit suicide. I just don't believe it!''

CHAPTER 16

TAMAR WAS SCREAMING. THERE WAS NOTHING NEW about that, nor about the language she was using. What was new was that she was getting back as good as she gave—and not from Uncle Wilmer.

"You crazy fool!" A second *smack* followed hard on the heels of the first one and Tamar gave a shriek of rage rather than pain. "What do you think you're doing?"

Thwack! "I hate you, you—" Tamar invoked a vocabulary she had never learned at Aunt Maddy's knee. "Get out of my life! Get out of my house! Now! Leave! Instantly!" This pressing invitation was followed by a shower of personal effects from the window of the room over the garage.

"Oh, no you don't!" *Whack!* "I'm not losing another camera to you raving maniacs!" *Smack!* "And this isn't *your* house, it's your father's."

Thwack! Crash! Smash! "You'll do as *I* say!"

"Oh well," Aunt Maddy sighed. "Thank heavens we never stored any antiques in that room."

A small vase came soaring through the open window and shattered at our feet. We moved back.

"I think we should leave them to it," Aunt Maddy

said reflectively. "I don't feel able to do anything about *that*."

You've done enough. I bit back the comment, although it was true. If Aunt Maddy had not blurted out her suspicions in front of Toy Boy, he might have gone back to London by now.

Unfortunately he was brighter than one tended to give him credit for being. It had taken him about thirty-five seconds to work out that, if the circumstances of Davina's death made even Aunt Maddy uneasy, they were unlikely to satisfy the police.

It was something I didn't want to think about. If Davina had not committed suicide, then someone had to be responsible for the accident. As with the slug pellets in the aspirin bottle, the wrong pills could not have got into the bottle by themselves. And it didn't make sense— not now.

Prior to Wanda-Lu's arrival, practically any member of the family might have wanted Davina out of the way— even me. She had not been particularly subtle about signaling the way she would deal with us when she was the Lady of the House. The living-in members of the family, Aunt Maddy and me, would be tossed out to make our own way in the world. Mrs. Keyes would be consigned to the dust heap. The step-children would find that their father was no longer willing to advance money to subsidize their little schemes. It was even possible that Davina would have her own nominees for family accountant, banker and solicitor. If Davina had become Lady Creighleigh, practically any one of us might have profited by killing her.

However, Wanda-Lu was the new Lady Creighleigh—

and that was that. Or so we had thought. The devil we knew had been ousted by the devil we didn't know. Not that Wanda-Lu was particularly devilish, but it was noticeable that she was beginning to assert herself more as the days went by.

"I hate you! I hate you! I hate you!" Tamar had never been shy about asserting herself. Right now, I was on her side. I didn't want Toy Boy lurking about with his Pentax and his Hasselblad trying to turn the situation into a major scandal. Our only hope was that Tamar would manage to throw him out. If any of the rest of us tried, he would jump to the conclusion that we had something to hide.

"I never want to see you again!"

"Well, that's all right, isn't it? I'm staying here and you're living over in the house. Just go back there and I'll try to keep out of your way."

Aunt Maddy and I withdrew still farther until we were out of earshot. The argument was extremely depressing—especially the fact that Tamar seemed to be losing.

"She needn't try to drag me into the middle of this." Aunt Maddy knew only too well the way Tamar's mind worked. "I'm not going to get involved. She brought him down by herself, she can get rid of him by herself."

As we neared the front door, Wanda-Lu appeared at an upstairs window and stared towards the garage in unabashed fascination as another piece of bric-à-brac flew through the air. Aunt Maddy looked from the upstairs window to the garage and sighed.

"Tamar really does take after her father," I said.

"I realize that more every day." Aunt Maddy winced as something shattered on the gravel drive. "I don't find the thought comforting. It's rather alarming, in fact.''

"At least this time Tamar's got someone who can hold his own with her." And perhaps the same could be said for Uncle Wilmer, too.

"I'm afraid that's not such a good thing—" Aunt Maddy broke off. We had entered the hallway and Wanda-Lu was now at the foot of the stairs, obviously waiting for us.

"Oh, there you are, uh, dear." Aunt Maddy had still not decided on how to address a sister-in-law younger than any of her nieces. "Everything all right?"

"Since you ask, Mag-da-len—" Wanda-Lu had no such qualms, she used Aunt Maddy's full name, pronouncing it in the American way, giving every syllable full value.

Aunt Maddy winced.

"Everything is not all right, Mag-da-len." Wanda-Lu didn't notice her sister-in-law's reaction. "Wilmer is in the library doing what he calls "instructing his solicitor" —and I don't mind telling you I'm not happy at all about those instructions."

"It *is* awkward, dear," Aunt Maddy murmured appeasingly.

"It is more than awkward," Wanda-Lu said firmly. "It is just about unendurable. I mean, I was prepared for stepchildren who were older than me—Wilmer explained that fairly and squarely. I can deal with that. They're fully grown and we don't have to see them all that often. Which suits me just fine—" She cast a censorious glance in the direction of the garage.

"Tamar was always the difficult one," Aunt Maddy apologized.

"Nobody else has exactly rushed to welcome me into the family, either." Wanda-Lu gave a shrug. "I didn't expect they would. I had a pretty good idea what I was walking into, but I figured it would be worth it because I'd have Wilmer—" Perhaps the look on our faces stopped her.

"Oh, I know what you're thinking," she said. She probably did; she seemed to have few illusions—except where Uncle Wilmer was concerned. "But you don't see Wilmer the way I do. He was the smartest, most fascinating man I'd ever seen—and I wanted him. I love that man, really love him. Getting married was his idea. I didn't ask that much. I just wanted to have his baby."

"Oh heavens!" Aunt Maddy was so shocked she forgot to be tactful. "You're not—?"

"Not yet," Wanda-Lu said grimly. "But I'm sure trying."

I said nothing. I could readily see how Uncle Wilmer might have been flattered out of his mind by Wanda-Lu's proposition. Especially since we had all cheered his departure from Little Puddleton by insisting upon his advancing years and impending decrepitude. No wonder he had insisted on marrying her and carrying her home in triumph to prove to us all that someone thought him a reasonably young and romantic figure.

"So you can see why I'm not too keen to have a strange child hanging around," Wanda-Lu said. "To tell the truth, I don't want Wilmer's attention distracted away from me."

I could see more than that. Suddenly I could see why Davina had died.

Someone else must have been aware of Wanda-Lu's dislike of childish competition and decided to take advantage of her insecurity. Another shot in the campaign to underline the fact that she was not wanted here.

No one could have foreseen that Uncle Wilmer would have wanted to assume permanent responsibility for Lynette in the event of Davina's death, but it was a fairly safe bet that he would have been willing to take her into the house for a few days—or a few weeks—if Davina were taken ill and unable to care for her.

In that case, Davina's death might have been an accident. It was possible that someone had meant to do no more than incapacitate Davina for a while, so that Lynette would have to move in over here. A small child underfoot while Wanda-Lu was trying to adjust to her new environment would inevitably make things more difficult for her. It was really quite a feasible plan.

Unfortunately it had gone wrong and Davina had died.

The results were the same—and even more final. Lynette was now in line to be a permanent member of the household—a rival to any children Wanda-Lu might produce. And Wanda-Lu was not happy about the situation. Not one bit.

"Little Lynette is a nice child," Wanda-Lu said, as though someone had disputed it. "Her own family *must* want her. I'm sure Wilmer will get in the most awful trouble if he goes on like this. Her Daddy will sue him, or something."

"I'm not so sure about that," Aunt Maddy said vaguely. "I believe I once heard something about the father having emigrated. New Zealand, I think, or possibly Canada."

"You mean they might not be able to find him?"

"Oh, eventually, I'm sure . . ."

"Eventually! You mean . . . years?"

"It's possible," Aunt Maddy admitted. "Once they've emigrated, unattached men do tend to move around a great deal. No fixed address and all that . . ."

"I see." Wanda-Lu's eyes narrowed. "And Wilmer knows all this?"

It wasn't really a question and our silence answered it. We stood there and looked at each other steadily, no one saying anything.

Then the front door slammed and Tamar hurled herself into our midst. That took care of the silence.

"Get rid of him!" she blazed at Aunt Maddy. "Make him go! Lock the door and don't let him in! If he has the nerve to come to the table, don't serve him any food!"

"He's your guest, Tamar," Aunt Maddy sighed. "You can't—"

"I can! I can! I *will*!" Tamar was unburdened by any qualms about hospitality. "He's not my guest any longer. He's got to leave!"

"Tamar—" Aunt Maddy said wearily; She had fought a long and losing battle trying to instill some principles into her wayward niece—"I really cannot allow—"

"If you don't, I'll do it myself!"

"I guess she will," Wanda-Lu said. "I haven't been here long, but I can't help noticing that you're pretty good at pulling the welcome mat out from under people's feet around here."

Involuntarily I thought of the slug pellets and wondered if Wanda-Lu had found out about them. Neither Aunt Maddy nor I had told her, but perhaps Mrs. Keyes had complained about our questioning her and had let the story slip out.

If Wanda-Lu knew, she must suspect Tamar of being the guilty party. Certainly it was the sort of childish trick Tamar was more likely to indulge in than any of the others. I wondered if I believed it myself. But would Tamar have tampered with Davina's pills? I decided I didn't believe it—Tamar specialized in throwing scenes, not doing things quietly. Besides, she had had her hands full with Toy Boy all weekend. She still had.

"Do you mean—?" Ignoring Wanda-Lu's remark, Tamar turned her hostility on Aunt Maddy. "Do you mean you *refuse* to do anything about it?"

"It's your problem." For once, Aunt Maddy let a little hostility of her own take over. "You never bothered to consider *our* feelings when you brought your. . . your Toy Boy down here. Now you're tired of him and you expect *me* to get rid of him for you. Well, you can think again!"

"You mean you won't?"

"I won't!"

"Then I'll tell my father—" Tamar whirled and ran towards the library. "*He'll* make you do something!"

"I wouldn't break in on him right now." Aunt Maddy went after her. "He won't be best pleased."

Wanda-Lu and I looked at each other and shrugged. "*How* old did Wilmer tell me my dear li'l step-daughter Tamar was?"

"Thirty-five."

"My Gawd!" Wanda-Lu grimaced heavenwards, obviously slipping into a better humor. "Whatever happened to that stiff upper lip we always heard you English had?"

She giggled slightly. " 'Course, having got to know Wilmer, I figured there was something wrong with that story. Come on.'' She linked arms with me and drew me towards the library. ''I want to hear what happens when she busts in on Wilmer. He isn't going to like it.''

Not entirely loath to see my Cousin Tamar get some sort of come-uppance, I allowed Wanda-Lu to pull me along. We arrived at the library door to find Aunt Maddy prudently waiting outside until the first blast had died away.

The force of her father's fury blew Tamar back to the threshold of the room. Uncle Wilmer advanced upon her, eyes blazing. In the background I could see the Triffid quivering.

''Am I to have no peace? Is my own business so paltry, so insignificant, that I should be constantly interrupted in order to deal with your tawdry little affairs? Is it nothing to you—?''

Tamar was over the threshold and backing across the drawing room, Uncle Wilmer still stalking her in full tirade. The rest of us stepped hastily out of their way. The Triffid appeared in the doorway, watching the scene incredulously. Perhaps he thought Uncle Wilmer was going to do her actual harm.

''. . . Is that the kind of fool you take me for?'' Uncle Wilmer wound up explosively.

In the sudden silence, we could almost hear debris falling.

''Well?'' Having achieved the desired response, Uncle Wilmer changed tack abruptly. ''Well? Well? What is it, then? I haven't got all night. What do you want?''

''I—I—'' Unnerved, Tamar began to stammer out her

request—no longer a demand. It had been a long time since she had been subjected to the full fury of one of her father's famous performances. She was not accustomed to being on the receiving end of someone else's temper and it had shaken her considerably.

"But I don't understand." Uncle Wilmer shook his head in a puzzled way as she finished. "Why do you come to me with these petty domestic problems? They're not my province." He gave her a sunny smile. "Ask your mother."

"I don't think that's funny!" Tamar flared.

"Neither do I." Wanda-Lu gave her bridegroom a long, level look, as though beginning to see him clearly for the first time. It was possible that further revelations of Uncle Wilmer's true character might accomplish what family malice could not.

"You must settle it between yourselves. I can't be bothered with trifles!" Uncle Wilmer turned and went back into the library, the Triffid drifting in his wake, still with an unbelieving expression. The door slammed shut behind them.

Tamar swung around to face Wanda-Lu uncertainly.

"Well . . ." Wanda-Lu said slowly. "There's just one li'l problem. I asked Danny Lora to take some wedding pictures for me and I don't think he's finished yet. So I guess we'll just have to let him hang around a while longer. Only, from here on in, he'll be *my* guest."

CHAPTER 17

"I WISH I DIDN'T HAVE TO LEAVE YOU LIKE THIS."
Aunt Flora brushed cheeks while Reggie loaded their
cases into the car. "I feel as though I were deserting
a—deserting ship. But Reggie has to get back to work
and I have a Committee Meeting tomorrow—"

"It's all right," Aunt Maddy said. "Don't worry
about it, Flora, we understand."

"Don't *you* worry," Aunt Flora said. "We'll clear our
schedules and be back to spend next weekend with you."
She appeared to think she was being consoling.

"Oh no!" Aunt Maddy gasped. "You mustn't think of
such a thing. We couldn't put you to all that trouble."
She had gone pale.

"No trouble at all," Aunt Flora assured her. "We'll be
back on Friday. That's a promise."

"Oh no." Aunt Maddy leaned against the door-jamb
weakly as the car swept down the drive. "That's all we
need."

"It's a reasonable question." Mrs. Keyes faced us, hands
on hips, defying us to deny it. "All I want to know is:
how much longer are they going to stay?"

"Dear heaven, I wish I knew!" Aunt Maddy said.

It was late Wednesday afternoon and all our nerves were badly frayed.

"All them people—not to mention the dogs." Mrs. Keyes was quivering with indignation. "I don't mind little Lynnie, but all them others is too much!"

"Godfrey left this morning," I pointed out. "And Jennifer hitched a lift back with Mr. Fortescue yesterday." Jennifer was showing a strong inclination to abandon Uncle Wilmer's bird-in-the-bush for the one in hand and I wished her every success.

"But they keep coming back," Mrs. Keyes complained. "How am I supposed to cook when I never know how many will be here for a meal? It isn't right."

She had a certain amount of justice on her side, although we hated to admit it.

"It's *her* that's the worst—and him over the garage. *They* aren't going—and half the time he doesn't come to meals. Although I will say for him, he's kept the rest of them off."

I was able to disentangle this fairly easily. The wave of press photographers had swept down on the village after the news about Uncle Wilmer's wedding had broken and Toy Boy, jealously guarding his own exclusive beat, had done some sort of deal with them to keep them at bay. Fortunately, a political scandal had erupted back in London and they had departed as rapidly as they had arrived, with the promise that Sir Wilmer and Lady Creighleigh would give them a proper interview soon.

"But it's all too much. I don't know as Mr. Keyes will let me keep working my fingers to the bone here like this—"

"If you're after more money," Aunt Maddy said, "you'll have to speak to Lady Creighleigh about it. She's in charge of all domestic matters now."

It was a palpable hit followed by a palpable pause as Mrs. Keyes tried to work out whether her position was strong enough to risk chancing her arm so soon. After all, Wanda-Lu had been in the house less than a week.

"She isn't here right now," Mrs. Keyes evaded, her glare showing what she thought of the way Aunt Maddy was hiding behind her new sister-in-law's skirts and refusing to come out and have a good fight.

"That's right. *Sir* Wilmer and *Lady* Creighleigh—" Aunt Maddy emphasized the titles slightly—"are in London. They're on some late-night television show tonight, so they'll be staying overnight. They'll be back tomorrow."

"*Newsmakers Tonight*," Mrs. Keyes supplied automatically, thereby losing points in the little game she and Aunt Maddy played. Mrs. Keyes was a deep-dyed snob and Uncle Sir Wilmer was the nearest she had ever come to celebrity. She would not relinquish her position here lightly, no matter how poorly she considered she was paid. In fact, her salary was higher than she might have earned anywhere within a radius of fifty miles—especially when her little eccentricities were taken into account.

"That's the show!" Aunt Maddy assumed an air of pleased surprise. "You'll be watching tonight, like the rest of us? We mustn't delay you, then. You'll want to finish up here so that you can get away early."

Mrs. Keyes was back in the kitchen before she knew what had happened to her . . .

We watched the program on the television set in my study. Lynette had been allowed to stay up late for it. She was still subdued and had taken to clutching Cromwell for comfort, carrying him around with her as other children carried a teddy bear. Cromwell was very good about it, obviously sensing her need. He curled in her lap now, uttering only a perfunctory growl as Tamar came into the room with Frou-Frou at her heels.

"Where's your ... friend?" Aunt Maddy asked.

"He's gone down to the pub, they'll all be watching it there." Tamar slumped into a chair and stared moodily at the TV set. "But I'm still not speaking to him." Frou-Frou gave Cromwell a guarded look and huddled close to Tamar's feet for protection. She had learned her lesson about Cromwell's claws.

Wanda-Lu photographed beautifully and, unfortunately, looked even younger than she was. When the camera turned to Uncle Sir Wilmer, the inevitable phrase that must have come to everyone's mind was: *cradle snatcher.*

Uncle Sir Wilmer beamed into the camera, extremely pleased with himself and making no bones about it. He had shown them all.

"Oh dear," Aunt Maddy clucked. "That suit is a disgrace. It's the same one he was wearing at his birthday party and it looked dreadful then, too. I must get all his things to the cleaners next week."

"Among the many triumphs and accomplishments of your distinguished life, Sir Wilmer," the compère smarmed, "which one do you consider—?"

Uncle Wilmer caught Wanda-Lu's hand before the question ended and swung it up over their heads in a boxing champion's salute. The studio audience went wild; he got the laugh he intended and the rest of the question was drowned by cheers.

"Quite so," the compère said. "And is it true, Sir Wilmer, that you may soon be presenting a major series of your own on Popular Economics on another Channel?"

"I wouldn't like to make a comment on that yet—" Uncle Wilmer's smile was all the comment they needed. "It's a bit early to say. Contracts to be ironed out and all that. It will be announced when the time is ripe. In fact—" he gazed fondly at Wanda-Lu—"there may be all sorts of announcements, in the fullness of time."

"The old fool!" Aunt Maddy exploded. "Why can't he keep his mouth shut? He'll start the Press off again."

"That's probably just what he wants. He's never been the shrinking violet type." My comment was not well-received.

"I know what I'd like to shrink!" Aunt Maddy said. She glanced at Lynette and amended carefully, "I'd like to shrink his head!"

"It could do with some shrinking," Tamar said. "He's been more big-headed than usual since that lecture tour."

"Wait until his own TV program starts," I said. "We'll have to widen the doors.

Wisely, the program directors had allowed Sir Wilmer to close the show, correctly estimating that he would be too hard an act for anyone to follow. The camera held on beaming faces as the credits began to crawl across the screen.

"That's all for tonight." Aunt Maddy pushed a button and the screen went dark. "Come on, Lynnie, time for bed."

"I don't want to," Lynette said. She scowled at the blank screen. "I want to watch the film."

"It's too late, Lynnie. You can hardly keep your eyes open now. It's way past your bedtime."

"No!" Lynette protested as Aunt Maddy pulled her to her feet. "No!" She stamped her foot experimentally; she had seen Tamar do that the other day. I hoped she wouldn't try throwing anything. She was learning bad habits in this family.

"I don't want to!" Her voice rose. Cromwell gave her a startled look and wriggled free of her arms, dropping to the floor for quieter parts of the house.

"There now, you've frightened Cromwell!" Tamar scolded. "Aren't you ashamed of yourself?"

Lynette burst into tears.

Aunt Maddy regarded Lynette with a strange expression for a moment, but there could be no doubt that Lynette's tears were genuine. Not because she had upset Cromwell, but because the bed she was being sent to was not her own, the house she was in was not her own; her mother was dead and nothing would ever be safe and familiar again. There must be so many tears stored up in her waiting for release that it was remarkable she had been as good as she had.

"Come along, Lynnie." Aunt Maddy stooped and picked her up. "We'll go downstairs and I'll make some hot chocolate for us." She carried the child from the room.

I wandered around the study, picking paper dolls up off the floor, removing a set of watercolor paints from my desk, retrieving a red rubber ball from the corner of a chair, trying to restore some sort of order. Trying to make the place seem like mine again.

Tamar watched me with amusement. "Now you're getting an idea," she said.

"What idea?"

"What it's like to have a cuckoo in the nest."

She was only getting at me because Toy Boy wasn't in range. I knew that, but she upset me just the same.

"Is that the way you've thought of me all these years?" It wasn't fair; they had all left home anyway by the time Uncle Wilmer had taken me into the house. I hadn't dispossessed anyone.

"You . . . Wanda-Lu . . , and now Lynette . . . what's the difference?" Tamar shrugged. "Father has some sort of *paterfamilias* complex. He should have been a Victorian with fourteen children and the house never quiet for a moment."

"It isn't very quiet now."

As though to prove it, the telephone rang. I picked up the extension on my desk. It was probably Uncle Wilmer checking to see how he had looked on the small screen. He expected us to take notes to help him improve future performances.

"Hello? Is that you, Pippa?" It was the Triffid. I was so pleased to hear a friendly—or at least neutral—voice after Tamar's sudden attack that I welcomed him more warmly than I might otherwise have done.

"Ian—how nice. Did you see Uncle Wilmer on *Newsmakers Tonight*?" I could think of no other reason he might be calling.

"No . . . was he on? I've been busy."

"You'd better not let him know that. He gets very upset if everyone doesn't cluster around the set and watch."

Tamar rose to her feet, still amused, still faintly malicious. "I'll let you have your private conversation," she
said. "But be careful and don't rush into anything.
Remember . . . the first time I got married, it was just to
get away from home."

"I have no intention—" I began indignantly. But she
was gone.

"What was that, Pippa?" I was confusing the Triffid
on the other end of the line.

"Nothing." He'd have been horrified if he'd known
what Tamar had just implied. "I was saying goodnight to
Tamar, that's all."

"Oh . . . has she gone now?" He did not approve of
Tamar and I found the thought did not upset me. I was
not so sure I approved of Tamar myself.

"All's clear," I assured him. "You can speak freely."

"Can I?" He was doubtful. "Are you sure there's no
one listening on any of the extensions?"

"*Really*, Ian!" I had meant it as a joke, but he was
taking it seriously.

"I want to talk to you. Privately. Before I have to
report to Sir Wilmer."

"Ian—what's the matter?"

"I don't know. I'm hoping you can tell me. How about
meeting me for lunch tomorrow? Sir Wilmer and Lady
Creighleigh are due to stop in at the office on their way
back from London and sign the new Wills. I'd rather not
see them—my father is back on duty and he can handle
that. Sir Wilmer would prefer him, anyway."

"Ian—?"

"You know the Black Lion? Meet me there at twelve-thirty. Take the bus, I'll drive you back after lunch and I can talk to Sir Wilmer then."

"Ian—what on earth is the matter? You've got to tell me at least something now. You can't leave me to wonder about it all night."

"I suppose not," he admitted reluctantly. "But I don't know what to make of it, not unless you can throw some light on it. I've found Hardy."

"Hardy?" For a moment, the name meant nothing to me, then I remembered. "Oh, you mean Lynette's father? Good!" I was unprepared for the relief that flooded through me. Was I really going to be so pleased to see the child leave? Would my cousins have felt the same about me if there had been any place else for me to go? "You mean he's back in England?"

"He never left," Ian said. "I don't know where everyone got the idea he'd emigrated. He's been here all along."

"All along? But why—?"

"Tomorrow," he said and rang off.

I wandered down to the kitchen to give Aunt Maddy the good news, but she wasn't there. Perhaps it was just as well. I couldn't have mentioned it in front of Lynette, anyway.

They had evidently just left. The saucepan for the hot chocolate had been washed and left on the draining board to dry, as had the two cups they had used.

Something about that tugged uneasily at my memory. I turned away, trying to leave the uneasiness behind me, but it followed me and kept nagging.

It was not until I was drifting off to sleep that it came to me. I closed my eyes and saw again two cups upside down on the draining board. The image was suddenly juxtaposed with another: two whisky glasses upside down on another draining board.

Davina's kitchen; Davina's draining board.

Someone had had a late night drink with Davina after she had gone home from our party. Someone had laced her drink with sleeping pills, returning later to leave the empty bottle by her bedside.

And Davina's ex-husband had never left England. Ian's words drifted back to me:

"He's been here all along . . ."

CHAPTER 18

IT WAS A GOLDEN DAY; THE SUN SPLASHED DOWN ON the multicolored canvas roofs of the stalls in the market place with Mediterranean abandon. The displays of fruit and vegetables were a lavish indication of the bumper harvest to come. Wanda-Lu would be seeing the countryside at its best as she and Uncle Wilmer drove back from London today. I hoped it would make up for her rain-sodden introduction to the country.

There was a bus stop right in front of the Black Lion but I got out a couple of stops before so that I could walk through the center of the Market Town savoring the smell and sight and sounds of market day. I loved country towns and villages and sometimes wondered if I could ever love London as much. In a half-hearted way, I had always thought that I might move to London for a couple of years when I came into my inheritance. Everyone should live in a metropolis at least once, if only to learn whether they really wanted to stay there.

Trifflin & Trifflin, Solicitors, had their offices on the other side of town looking out on a leafy Georgian square. If Ian Trifflin and I were to slide into a serious involvement, I could live here and have the best of town and country life and still be close enough to Little Puddleton to visit the family frequently.

Then I cursed my Cousin Tamar for putting such an idea into my head in the first place.

Ian had booked a table by the window at the upstairs dining room of the Black Lion and was waiting for me. We ordered the speciality of the day and wine. When the waitress had left, I didn't bother with small talk.

"What's going on? Have you found out?"

"I'm not sure," he said. "I was hoping *you* could tell *me*."

"What do you mean?"

"Acting upon Sir Wilmer's instructions," he began formally, "I contacted the late Mrs. Hardy's solicitors pursuant to—"

"Oh, come off it," I interrupted. "You're not issuing a tort!"

He winced. "Actually, torts aren't—"

"You know what I mean. Speak English!"

"I told them I wanted to begin trying to trace Mr. Hardy. They didn't know what I was talking about. It seemed he'd never been missing. Where did everyone in your family get the idea that he had emigrated?''

"I don't know. We just always thought so. I suppose Davina must have told us originally.''

"I don't know what she'd do that for—''

"Lots of women invent stories about their past. It helps them to live with it.''

"Not just women—'' He looked as though he might be remembering a few cases.

"Anyway—'' he pulled himself back to the matter in hand—"I contacted Hardy by telephone and tried to set up an appointment to see him. He wasn't too keen on the idea. Kept wanting to know what it was all in aid of. In the end, I had to tell him a bit of the problem. He'd heard about Davina's death, of course, but he didn't seem to realize that anything might be expected of him—''

"I'd like to be sure he didn't know more than any of us about Davina's death,'' I said grimly. "I suspect he may have been the first to know.''

"What's that?''

"I'll tell you later. Go on.''

"Well, before mentioning Sir Wilmer's idea, I thought it would be best to try to discover if he had any plans of his own for the child. That was really why I wanted to see him. These delicate matters are best handled face to face . . .''

The waitress appeared beside us with our steaming platters. The restaurant was filling up, market traders and shoppers now having to share tables, cheerful and laughing with the camaraderie of market day. Out of the corner of my eye I spotted a couple laden with carrier bags heading purposefully for the two empty seats at our table.

"I told him that Lynette was now her father's responsibility—" Ian had seen them, too, he spoke rapidly, trying to get the information over to me before we had to share the table and switch to neutral topics. The Black Lion had not been such a good idea, after all.

"I told him that Sir Wilmer was looking after Lynette *pro tem* but that he himself would have to make arrangements for her future care, unless he was satisfied with the *status quo* and—" Ian bared his teeth at the two new-comers as they pulled out the chairs after a perfunctory question, and finished in a rapid undertone—

"And he laughed! He broke into quite maniacal laughter and hung up on me!"

"Hold it!" Toy Boy shouted as we got out of the car.

Instinctively we froze—until the click of the camera released us and we realized that it was only Toy Boy busily trying to justify his presence again.

"Is Sir Wilmer back yet?" I asked as we brushed past him.

"Due any minute now," he said cheerfully, making some mysterious adjustment to his camera. It was the Hasselblad, I noticed, the one he had identified as the most expensive. I could only hope, for his sake, that he was not going to antagonize Uncle Wilmer enough to endanger it. "Thought you was him—were them—" he corrected.

"We're not." Ian stated the obvious as we dashed for the front door. It was clear that Toy Boy, well aware of his *persona non grata* status, was keeping clear of the house until he could enter with Wanda-Lu, reminding everyone that he was her guest.

Lynette was skipping rope in the front hall. I noted absently that both Uncle Wilmer and Wanda-Lu would have just cause for annoyance as soon as they got home. Uncle Wilmer was not pleased with Wanda-Lu's decision to extend personal hospitality to Toy Boy and Wanda-Lu was far from pleased with Lynette's presence. It was too bad they couldn't have managed a trade-off instead of a stalemate.

The green baize door at the end of the hall swung open and Mrs. Keyes stood there. "Would you like—?" she began ingratiatingly, then stopped.

"Oh, it's just you." The fawning expression slipped from her face. She turned and went back to the kitchen.

"Mrs. Keyes, you promised we could make gingerbread men—" Lynette dropped her rope and went after her.

I picked up the skipping rope and wound it around its handles. Strange that I had never noticed before how much more work there was to do with a child around, just picking up after her kept one busy. It really was most unfair of Uncle Wilmer to wish it on Wanda-Lu and Aunt Maddy. He wasn't the one who'd have to keep the place tidy.

"I must get on to Hardy again." Ian looked after Lynette. "That laughter was no kind of answer. We'll need a written agreement—if he does agree. But—" the question still perplexed him—"why did he laugh like that?"

"Oh, Pippa, it's you." Aunt Maddy came in from the garden, carrying a trug of freshly-cut flowers. "I heard the car and I thought—"

"Sir Wilmer and Lady Creighleigh stopped at the

office," Ian said. "They ought to be here in time for tea."

"Thank you, dear, that's just what I wanted to know." Aunt Maddy disappeared into the cupboard under the stairs to select a vase.

I realized suddenly that the flowers Davina had brought over for the birthday party had disappeared after we had found her dead. It was typical of the smoothly unobtrusive way Aunt Maddy had always run the household. Anything potentially disturbing was quietly swept away. There were neither roses nor peonies among the fresh flowers Aunt Maddy was now arranging in the vase. Nothing that might raise unhappy memories and distress Uncle Wilmer. I wondered if Wanda-Lu would ever be able to run the household with such efficiency.

Tamar was in the drawing room frowning over a sketch-pad, swatches of material on the arm of her chair. I wondered how much longer she could afford to neglect her own business to indulge in the sheer spite of trying to outstay Toy Boy. When you're decorating interiors, you have to visit those interiors occasionally—it's the least the client expects.

"Pippa, dear . . . and Ian." She gave me a meaning smile. "Did you have a nice lunch?"

"Very nice, thanks." I would not give her the satisfaction of seeing that she had annoyed me. "And you're keeping busy, I see."

That brought back her familiar frown. She picked up one of the swatches and matched it against something in the sketch, making it clear that she was too busy to waste time on me.

I grimaced at Ian and led him through into the library.

It was quiet in there. Cromwell was asleep, stretched out along the front of one of the bookshelves. He opened one eye and chirruped a greeting, then went back to sleep again.

"Lunch was too good," I said. "I could curl up and go to sleep myself."

"So could I." Ian looked at me thoughtfully. "However, circumstances being as they are, perhaps we ought to settle for a stroll in the garden instead."

When we got back, Uncle Wilmer and Wanda-Lu had arrived and tea was being served in the drawing room.

Aunt Maddy was pouring; she filled cups and passed them to us with a benign smile. As we took them, I was conscious of the click of a camera again. I looked over to the corner where Toy Boy was crouching.

"That's great," he said, straightening up. "Maybe I'll take up a sideline: funerals and weddings a speciality."

Uncle Wilmer frowned. I was conscious that I was frowning, too. It really was time Toy Boy left; he had long since outstayed his precarious welcome. I glanced over at Wanda-Lu, wondering if even she might be beginning to think that his jokes were in poor taste, but she did not appear to have heard him.

Tamar was studiously ignoring him, dividing her attention between her sketch-pad and Frou-Frou, who was waltzing on hind leg, begging tit-bits.

Lynette was gleefully helping to feed Frou-Frou, glancing anxiously at Aunt Maddy every now and again, as though expecting a reprimand for spoiling the dog. Aunt Maddy pretended not to notice.

Cromwell, lured by the clink of china, sauntered in

from the library to demand and get a saucer of milk. It was a quiet domestic scene, typical of a peaceful late summer afternoon.

Yet Uncle Wilmer looked around and appeared dissatisfied. "When will Godfrey be back?" he demanded.

"Godfrey and Jennifer will be down tomorrow for the weekend... again," Aunt Maddy sighed. "So will Flora and Reggie."

Uncle Wilmer nodded, not quite satisfied.

"I thought you came over awfully well last night." I hurried to placate him. "And Wanda-Lu looked lovely."

"So I hear, so I hear." Uncle Wilmer began to smile. "They were telling us that after the show. Seemed to think it had gone very well. Everyone thought Wanda-Lu looked lovely."

"That's more than could be said for you." Aunt Maddy sniffed. "That suit is a disgrace? It looks as though you'd slept for a week on a park bench in it."

"That is true, Wilmer," Wanda-Lu said. "I think I'm gonna make that the first thing I nag you about. It's because you stuff everything into your pockets like a little boy and never empty them. Why, I'll just bet—" She advanced on him and dived for his top pocket, fishing into it before he could protest.

"There!" she pulled the handkerchief free, sending a shower of ticket stubs to the floor like wedding confetti. "Just look—there's your Amtrack ticket, and the tickets for that show we saw at Theatre-in-the-Round when we were courting, and I guess every bus ticket you ever had since you first got that suit."

Laughing, Uncle Wilmer stooped and helped her gather up the tickets, gazing at them reminiscently. He was unprepared when she swooped on another pocket.

"I've been dyin' to do this for ages!" She pulled out the contents of a side pocket. "We're gonna have a real old-fashioned clear-out and get you lookin' respectable again."

Uncle Wilmer had stopped laughing. He made an abortive snatch at the things in her hand but she danced away from him, sorting through them.

"The receipt from that funny li'l hotel we stayed at in Maryland and—Oh, Wilmer, you are a disgrace! Here's a card from one of your presents. How can we send thank-you notes if we don't know who gave you the things?" She smoothed the crumpled envelope and pulled out what was inside. It was not a card.

"Whatever's this?" She unfolded it and scanned it quickly, the mischief dropping from her as she read. "It—it's a Birth Certificate . . . for Lynette. And written here along the side, it says, "Perhaps Pippa should ask for an accounting, too." Wilmer, what does this mean? Wilmer?"

"Lynette, leave the room," Uncle Wilmer said in a strange voice.

"No! No! No!" Lynette shrieked. "It's mine! It's for me—she said so!" She darted forward and snatched the piece of paper from Wanda-Lu. "Let me see!"

"We'd all like to see it." Aunt Maddy reached out and deftly removed the paper from Lynette's hand.

Lynette screamed with outrage and burst into tears.

"Well, she's sure got your temper, Wilmer," Wanda-Lu said thoughtfully.

"Wanda—" Uncle Wilmer started forward, but Wanda-Lu backed away from him.

"Hold it!" Toy Boy was frantically snapping pictures. "This is great! Just turn this way! Lynnie! Go give Daddy a great big kiss, Lynnie!"

"Stop that! Stop it!" Uncle Wilmer rounded on Toy Boy, someone on whom he could safely expend his fury. "No pictures!" He grabbed for the camera.

"Oh no! You're not smashing another one!" Toy Boy struggled to keep it away from his grasp. "Not the Hasselblad!"

"Use one of those pictures and I'll smash you!" Uncle Wilmer threatened. He had a hold on the camera now and fought to possess it with demoniacal fury. He could only vent his rage by smashing something right now.

"Not the Hasselblad!" They thrashed about the room. Tamar screamed. Frou-Frou ran behind the sofa to join Cromwell.

"Wilmer, stop it!" Aunt Maddy shouted. "Tamar—make that boy behave! Wilmer—!"

They crashed into the drinks trolley, sending it flying. Both were determined on possession of that camera.

"Not the Hasselblad!" Toy Boy kept shouting, as though it were a battle cry.

After his first outburst, Uncle Wilmer fought silently and with a savagery that blinded one to his age. Toy Boy was battling as with an equal—a contemporary. What else could he do if he wanted to save his precious camera? Uncle Wilmer was determined on destruction.

"Not the—" Toy Boy got sole control of the camera and gave Uncle Wilmer a push.

Uncle Wilmer fell to the floor and did not get up.

Perhaps it was better so. Perhaps it was what Uncle Wilmer had intended all along.

Toy Boy backed away, aghast at what he had done. "I told you—" he defended himself wildly to Tamar, to us all.

"I told you he was barking mad!"

CHAPTER 19

"VERY BAD," REGGIE SAID. "VERY BAD ALL AROUND." He exchanged a long look with Aunt Flora and slipped out of the room. There was going to be something he did not want to hear—or was it something that he didn't want to explain?

The funeral was over and we were all gathered in the library, instinctively shunning the drawing room with its after-image of Uncle Wilmer stretched out upon the rug.

Almost all, that is. Ian Triffling was by my side and I was glad to have him there. He had been an unexpected tower of strength in dealing with the police—although perhaps I should have expected it, remembering how capably he had dealt with fire.

Tamar, however, was alone, dressed in black, looking more solemn than I had ever seen her. Perhaps she was belatedly growing up. She would not be seeing Toy Boy again—none of us would. We had bought his silence by promising our own. If we had told the police what had really happened, if any of the family had wanted to be nasty about it, Toy Boy might have found himself facing, at best, a charge of involuntary manslaughter. We had told the police that Uncle Wilmer had tripped over Frou-Frou, crashed into the drinks trolley as he fell heavily and . . . a sad accident with tragic consequences.

There was no reason the police should not believe it. They were aware that Sir Wilmer Creighleigh had recently returned from a strenuous lecture tour and they knew that he had undergone considerable stress since his return. Hadn't we all?

"I can't believe it—" Godfrey shook his head groggily. "*Father* killed Davina? Father? And Lynette is—" he choked—"our half-sister?"

"I'm afraid so," Aunt Maddy sighed. "I never suspected it until we had Lynette living here day and night. Then I began to notice little traits. Things that weren't noticeable when Davina used to take her home before she got too tired. Most children have tantrums when they're overtired, but there was something *familiar* about Lynette's." Her eyes flicked across Tamar. "I tried to convince myself that it was just association, bad example, but . . ."

"But you didn't say anything," Jennifer accused.

"What was there to say? The idea was just beginning to form at the back of my mind. Perhaps, after a bit more observation, I might have . . ."

"No wonder Davina expected Father to marry her," Godfrey said. "She had every right to expect it."

"Her mistake was in thinking that she could blackmail him into it just the same." I remembered the scene that had ended the birthday party. "No wonder he had a fit

when he opened that envelope. He must have known then
that there was only one way to keep her quiet—and get
custody of Lynette, as well.''

"But why did she wait so long?'' Godfrey asked.
''Why didn't she push for marriage earlier?''

"I can answer that,'' Ian said. ''I've talked to Hardy
again—a more sensible conversation this time. He knew
the child wasn't his and he was furious about it. He
refused to give Davina a divorce. She had to wait out the
five years before she could file for one herself. She
wasn't really divorced when she moved next door, she
only said she was. The real divorce only came through a
few months ago.''

"It was a mistake for her to move so close. Uncle
Wilmer got too good a view of her. He'd gone off the
idea by the time she was free. He was probably wondering
how he could get out of it when he met—'' I broke off.
The widow had been so quiet I'd forgotten she was still
in the room.

"When he met me,'' Wanda-Lu finished for me.

There was an embarrassed silence.

Cromwell gave a querulous cry and rubbed his head
against Wanda-Lu's hand; she resumed stroking him
absently. He looked at my cousins suspiciously, but they
had left their dogs in London today.

"Aunt Maddy.'' There was one thing I had to know, a
painful subject she had evaded ever since that nightmare
afternoon. I couldn't go through the rest of my life not
knowing. ''Aunt Maddy, that note about *me* on the Birth
Certificate. Does that mean—?''

"Don't be silly, Pippa,'' Aunt Maddy said. ''Of course

Wilmer wasn't your father. I don't know how you could have got such an idea."

"But that note—" I began to relax inwardly. I had not really thought so, but it was difficult to know what to think. So much had happened—and so quickly.

"Ah yes, that note," Aunt Maddy sighed. "It said that perhaps you should ask for an accounting—and I'm afraid it meant exactly that." She looked around, as though for help, but Reggie had escaped. "You know Wilmer had been handling your estate—"

"But everything's all right there," I said. "I've seen statements—"

"Oh, you haven't *lost* any of your inheritance," Aunt Maddy said quickly. "Not in that way. Wilmer wasn't dishonest but, when all that money fell into his hands . . . I don't know, Pippa, I just don't know. To tell the truth, I've never wanted to know."

"But you have a pretty good idea of what happened." Ian was not prepared to let the matter drop. "I think you'd better tell us."

"I think . . . it gave him a chance to test his theories. He'd never had much money before; there were the children and the school fees and all the domestic expenses. Also, he had the feeling that Life was passing him by, I suppose, and he hadn't accomplished nearly what he'd intended. It didn't seem to him that he was doing anything wrong. He'd have made it up to you, Pippa, if he'd lost any of your money, but he didn't."

"No," I agreed. "He really proved that he knew what he'd been talking about all those years, didn't he?"

"That's it," she said gratefully. "I'm sure it didn't seem wrong to him. It was just suddenly the children were grown out of the way and that expense was done with. I was here, of course, and so were you, but he could take care of us out of his salary. It must have seemed to him that, for once in his life, he had some spare money to play around with. And, as soon as he made the first killing in the Stock Market, he put back all he'd taken out of your account and just went on after that using his winnings.''

"Pippa's winnings, you mean," Ian said sternly. "Technically, all of this—" his gesture encompassed the room, the house, the garden—"all this was bought with her money. It belongs to—"

"Oh, don't be such a—a *solicitor!*" I cried. "It doesn't matter. I've still got plenty." Another thought occurred to me, one I couldn't resist flinging at my cousins, one final scoring off to make up for all the little snubs across the years.

"Except—" I stared directly at Tamar—"it means I'm not a cuckoo in the nest, after all, doesn't it?" I looked at the other cousins. "My money provided the nest!"

Lynette had been the cuckoo Uncle Wilmer had dropped in Mr. Hardy's nest and no wonder he had reacted with such bitter amusement when Ian had told him that Davina was dead and he was expected to take responsibility for the child. Poor Lynette—thank heaven we had been able to send her to stay with Mrs. Keyes for the day.

"But *some* of the money must have been Father's," Tamar wailed. "He wouldn't have used *just* Pippa's! Where's Uncle Reggie? He was Father's accountant. He *must* be able to sort it out. Ohhh—" her voice rose in a shriek of rage. "How could Father *do* such a thing to us?"

"I don't think you realize," Aunt Maddy said slowly, "that the selfishness of those at the . . . far end of life . . . can be more ferocious, more terrifying, than that of the merely young and ambitious. You'll have other chances. You have time to live down your mistakes, but for us—for Wilmer—it was a case of . . . perhaps the last chance. I don't think you can blame him entirely for . . . for grabbing at anything and everything Life offered . . ."

"Like me," Wanda-Lu said. "It's funny, isn't it? All those awful jokes I had to take about choosin' to be an old man's darlin' instead of a young man's fool. And it turns out I'm a fool, after all."

"Wilmer was the fool!" Aunt Flora said savagely. "He always was a fool!"

"What—what are you going to do now?" Godfrey asked Wanda-Lu warily.

"I haven't had time to think." Wanda-Lu shrugged. "I guess I'll get to keep my title, won't I? That's more than most women will ever have. For the rest of it—"

"You must stay on here," I said. "It's too soon for you to make any decisions. After a few months you'll have a better idea of what you want to do."

"Maybe." She shrugged again. "But I'd rather not have anything to do with that kid. I'm just glad Wilmer never had time to do anything legal about her. I'm sorry—but that's just the way it is."

"Of course it is," Aunt Maddy said. "I wouldn't think of burdening you with her. Burdening any of you . . . but the child *is* a Creighleigh." She straightened and threw back her shoulder. "I'm strong and healthy, good for another ten or twenty years, I hope. I ought to be able to last until Lynette is of an age to look after herself. I'll take care of her until then. Although—" she looked around—"perhaps not here. The place is too big. If we sell it—Sorry, Pippa . . . I forgot."

"That's all right," I said. "The whole thing is a mess, but don't worry—my solicitor will take care of it." I threw him a reckless vote of confidence. He did not appear to appreciate it. "Ian will sort it out."

"It won't be easy." He gave me an enigmatic look, then seemed to find the silver lining. "It will take quite a considerable length of time—and there will have to be a great many long and intimate conferences with . . . my client."

THERE'S NO FOOL LIKE AN OLD FOOL.
OR A DEAD ONE.

It's a house of fools. Thirty-five-year-old Tamar acts more like sixteen, accompanied by her boyfriend, an adolescent "Toy Boy" who has his own reason for partaking of the Creighleighs' hospitality. In the kitchen Mrs. Keyes makes life miserable for everyone, while Godfrey Creighleigh and his sister, Jennifer, busily count the money their father will leave them in his newly revamped will. A new will? Certainly something big is up on the occasion of Sir Wilmer's triumphant return from America. After all, the old boy has summoned his banker and his solicitor to the family gathering. Unfortunately for all, the surprise Sir Wilmer has in store can make anyone look like a fool. Or a killer...

MARIAN BABSON is one of Great Britain's leading mystery writers. A former secretary of the Crime Writers Association, she has penned over thirty mysteries acclaimed for their remarkable diversity and inventiveness. Ms. Babson has won Britain's Poisoned Chalice and was nominated for a Golden Dagger, Britain's equivalent of the Edgar.

"Books of marvellous versatility and freshness...(with) flashes of delicious humor.... Marian Babson's crime novels have gone from strength to strength."
— *Twentieth Century Crime and Mystery Writers*

A SELECTION OF THE DETECTIVE BOOK CLUB

36008

0 70993 00450 7

ISBN 0-446-36008-2

WARNER BOOKS
A Time Warner Company
COVER PRINTED IN U.S.A.
© 1991 WARNER BOOKS